SPIKES

Finding Hope in a Broken Heart

J . R-. K N O X

PAGE PUBLISHING, INC.
New York, NY

First originally published by Page Publishing, Inc. 2019

ISBN 978-1-64584-434-1 (Paperback)
ISBN 978-1-64584-435-8 (Digital)

Printed in the United States of America

In Memory of Rhuarama "Mother" Knox. You were truly a mother to all and the heart and soul of our community. I am endlessly appreciative of the wisdom you imparted on that hard-headed boy, whom has now become a man. Your light continues to guide me.

To Jon & Jessica

Many blessings to you
and your family.

With Love,

[signature]

Chapter 1

IN DEATH, I SHALL LIVE

How does it feel? The treachery. The deceit. The feeling of loss. Losing my uncle was all that and more. He was a crutch, a punk, a saint, immoral, but most importantly, unforgettable. I don't like to say that he was taken from me, oh no, it needs to sound worse. He was stolen from me. Like the SWAT team of life had decided it was his time. They couldn't do the job themselves. They needed to send in a henchman…a silent one. But I can't keep staring at myself. What is being angry going to solve anyway? I think I'll just walk out this room, look everyone in the eye, and put on a fake one. Making everyone happy is my calling as they see it.

Everyone has a role in their family. My uncle was my confidant, my security blanket, and still remained a family albatross. Oh and my mom—she is the opinionated one. Never lets the facts get in the way of being right. I have an aunt who lets her wealth do the talking, but she is always able to drop a nugget of thought. My favorite is, "In order to be a champion, you must accept the challenge." That is what I aim to do.

I prepare for my soul to drop as I surf upon the social wave. My artificial self begins producing conversations from a data bank of memories as I dart around the room. For a moment, I left life. I'm supposed to be the happy one, the one people could look at, and just with that look, they know things are not so bad. Where is that look?

Why can't I muster it? Authenticity evades me like the plant in the corner of the living room.

"*Heyyy!* It is so good to see you! How are you?" The bloodhound of the family has found me.

"I'm as good as I can be Aunt Terry." Hiding emotions are pointless around her.

"I know you were real close with him. My brother was good at pulling people in just to push them away. God rest his soul."

A semblance of controllable thought creeps back to me on the level of a baby speaking its first words.

"Do you really think he is at rest Aunt Terry? With God or anyone else?"

"Of course…" She pauses. "That's an odd thing to say coming from you. Since when did you begin doubting the power of God?"

"I'm n—"

"Don't you ever doubt the abilities of our Lord and Savior! The day you begin that is the day your faith is gone!"

The biblical remedial tongue lashing was not without its merit given my by-the-book past. This feeling I have as a result of my uncle's passing is different. Why does this resolve I have feel void of feeling? There is a peace to it.

Dinner is filled with the glorious sounds of clacking silverware, the longer it goes, the less likely this enjoyable hymn will be inter-rupted. This family has its ways of zigging when you think they will zag. I look over the elegant table setting. This is only done for com-pany. Why? I look at the apropos attire of my cousin, who truly believes he is a magnet for the opposite sex, whether they are married or not. His eyes feverishly move to the spouses of his two brothers, waiting for one to choose him. Clueless children sit within the room, two arm lengths away, and my plate sits here…untouched.

"You need to eat, cuz," Bud says.

A smirk grows on my face as I hone in on an easy target.

"You don't need to eat, cuz."

The remark drew eyes from Aunt Terry.

"Don't let your Mother's cooking go to waste boy. Your Mom cancelled two catering orders and took time off to do this."

"But why, Aunt Terry…" This doesn't feel like me. Why am I being so mindlessly inquisitive? "Sorry, I'm just crazy. Yes, ma'am, I'm sorry."

"All right then," as she expresses an authoritative nod.

As dinner concludes, the house slowly becomes less dense. I feel a vibration, followed by a familiar tone. It was the most alive I have been in a while.

"You finally answered, dude. I'm coming to get you. We have somewhere to be."

I always enjoyed it when he played his orange card. Being a believer in *True Colors*, I valued when Sedrick's personality shines. Although counter to my step-by-step approach and tempered countenance, he knows right when to strike.

"Okay, where are we going?"

"Somewhere I should have taken you a while ago! Be ready in ten minutes, I gotta get right so it's going to take a little longer."

As much as he overdoes his fragrances, we are on the same page when it comes to places to let off some steam. I never needed to ask Sedrick the style of dress for the occasion. We were synched! I don't know if it was his tone, the time of day, or some other random possible coincidence that clued me in.

I move quickly to my room and pull out the perfect fit for the occasion. I pop the cork on a fresh pair of shoes and take care of some quick maintenance before I head out the door waiting on him. Immediately, I thought I should have brought a jacket, but I had braved worse before.

Sedrick pulls up in his car that had a more polished look than normal.

"You ready to do this?" Sedrick bounces as he excitedly exclaims. "I think you are really going to like this place."

"I hope you are right."

"Sorry about your loss, man. Your unc was special. Cool guy and lived life like it should be lived."

I'm not quite sure how I feel about that comment, so I quickly dismiss it.

"What's new with you and Briana?"

"Who?" he smiles as he changes the subject. "Have you decided your next move? You have your degree, you have a steady job *and…*" Sedrick produces a rare pause in his thoughts before continuing. "Your uncle might have left you a lot of money."

I'm sure my look is giving away my thoughts. Maybe I should let it go as a Sedrick-being-Sedrick moment, but not this time.

"I'm going to completely dismiss the timing and thoughtlessness of my feelings with that comment, Sed. My uncle was never rich. I don't know why you would think that. He didn't leave anyone anything but heartache. Don't get me wrong, my uncle was a G! I connected with him on so many levels… There's nothing left man…"

Why am I into my feelings now? I need to stop this mess and change the subject.

"So Sed, tell me about where we are going."

"Eh, I'm sorry about bringing up your uncle."

"Forget about it, it's over. So how live is this spot you're taking me to."

Sedrick lit up like a starved individual at a buffet.

"Let's just say it will take you there."

His wink was a sure sign this was going to be a night I would not forget.

Chapter 2

AN OMINOUS JOURNEY

The outside of this crack shack can be likened to a place that would be filled with clandestine gazes, suits, concealed weapons, and old-school, scantily clad guy ornaments. Shifty characters are positioned with a symmetrical distance between them. The attempt to be obscure is laughable. I would have never expected this to be in this glitzy area of the city. Leave it to Sedrick to find sketchy in the most abnormal of places.

"C'mon, man! Now the fun begins." Sedrick's comments do not provide comfort or fear. They simply linger in my consciousness as I analyze my surroundings and reassess what fun is for Sedrick.

The inside of this place contradicts my original thoughts! I never thought I would be caught in a moment when slacks and a dress shirt would feel like beach attire. I could sense the money in the room. One could buy a house or a small piece of land with one of their accessories. Strangely and happily, I am going unnoticed. Eyes collide without judgement. Smiles are returned and the mood is inviting while still being quite unsettling as I get my bearings. The phrase, "Act like you've been there" is always tougher in practice. What grabs my attention the most are their faces. *Pure joy*! Their eyes search for a different wonder, more so than judgement. Most everyone is reveling in the ambiance. It is a massive open room with light rhythm and blues playing in the background. I see a few open corridors and rooms on the side. People of all shades are here. How did Sedrick find this place? Speaking of Sedrick, he is heading for one of the theater-leveled lounge areas. He knows this place, so it is smart to follow.

"I would like to introduce you to your friends," Sedrick states with a non-regal bow.

My curiosity and wonder disappear momentarily as I lay eyes on this surprise. "Ladies…fellas, wow! Tell me you didn't come here because Sedrick asked?"

"That's exactly why we are here," Haven says.

"Yeah, we knew about your uncle, but when Sed told us you needed to get out and just cut loose, I wasn't going to miss that," Tory inserted.

"Oh, so Sedrick thought I needed a night out. That's what this is." It makes sense that Sedrick is looking away right now. He knows he was wrong for that, but that is why we vibe so well together. Being in each other's thoughts is status quo.

"We family, man, I'm always looking out for you," Sedrick interjects as a smile leaks across his face. "At least most of the time. But listen to this. There is something real unique that goes on here that I think you can be a part of and appreciate."

Sedrick waves me on, and now we are heading to the bar. He orders his typical and said that he was buying for me tonight. This was a nice change.

"Let me tell you, they have a game here that is crazy man. You won't believe it."

"Well, I didn't believe this place would be this nice on the inside either."

"Haven is a master at it, I'm aight, Tory is trash, and I think you'll be really good," Sedrick states with convincing confidence.

"So what is the game?"

The drinks arrive before he can answer. Of course, now he is raising his glass. I can't keep him on topic.

"I would like to propose a toast to Darren."

"Sed, get down man, you don't need to make a scene." My pleading went nowhere. When Sed wants to make something happen, he will. If only he could channel that into staying committed to that something.

"To Darren, the best friend I could ever have and the best Spikes player I have ever met and you will *ever* see!"

The reception he received catches me off guard. A passionate loud roar has come out of this swank crowd. It is reverberating around the room. There is more to this than what I originally thought. My heart is sinking and anxiety invades my body. The stranger's cheers are swiftly dissipating. Sedrick smiles while I wonder what just happened and what the heck is Spikes?

"Now that's an introduction to the game, D." Sedrick seems unabashed by my distraught look and soaked in that fleeting moment a little too much for my liking.

"What the hell was that, Sed? You threw me out there like—"

"Chill my dude, everything is cool. When you finally get a taste of this, you will want to be in every tournament!"

Sedrick casually detonates his comments as if I am already entered into a tournament. I know my boy and I are close, but dang. Sed hasn't led me astray before, so maybe this is about control or lack thereof. Our established friendship and my decision to tail him to this place entitle a little leash. He may know something that I don't. I must admit, I was briefly enjoying myself and that's because of Sed. Maybe I have gone a little wayward with my uncle's passing. I'll just keep my eyes open and see where this night leads me. Sometimes it is good to get lost in the moment.

"Okay...so where is this mythical game played? There's no room in here for another game."

You would think I just offered up a million dollars with Sedrick's reaction. He swells with pride just thinking about me going with this idea.

A beaming Sedrick responds, "I'll show you."

Weaving past the bar, we make our way into an equally sized room that had more pool tables than people. The mood here feels less welcoming than the other, but I'll shake that off for it being a new experience. As we walk by, I overhear four people having conversations in two different foreign languages. The craftsmanship of the pool tables are intense and inviting. I have never seen pool tables this elaborate before. There are multiple games taking place but spaced out from one another. If the look on the player's faces is what we have to look for, I want no part of it. I can taste the tension in the room and the onlookers don't make it any better.

Sedrick whispers, "You will never see officials decked out in Alexander Amosu suits anywhere, but here."

"I'm assuming those are expensive suits, but officials? Seems a little extra."

"Yes, they are monitoring the game making sure everything is done by the rules. When you are aiming for a particular client, you need to look the part."

"Then why are you here? And we are definitely not living up to the dress code of most."

"Haha, you letting the jokes go now. That's good. I'm glad you got that bad one out of the way. Maybe you're finally loosening up."

"Really, Sed, it's pool man, how difficult can it be? And why are we whispering all of a sudden?"

"This is Spikes my dude! It has pool concepts but a distinctive cutthroat flair in the name of competition. That is why you see the people that are not playing on the side. With the money being thrown around, you gotta have someone to regulate this."

"Man, they are probably just tired of gambling and are waiting for the next game." Of course, I'm not completely sold. Mama didn't raise no fool. I can just hear my Aunt Terry telling me that. She always wants me to be sharp. No matter the cocktail of emotions I have, I'm mentally intact.

"Do me a favor, bro…don't talk for a minute; you killing me. Some of those 'people' either have a wager on the game or they own the product, you know what I'm saying?" Sedrick clearly wants me to take this seriously.

My comment was a swing and a miss. Let me look a little closer at what I'm dealing with. Analyze the differences between them. I will have to table my personal study for a later date. For now, I need to know more.

"They pay these folks to play this?"

"Yes, and it is *big* money man, for real. There's a tournament coming up in a few months. It's going to be like March Madness, I'm telling you."

"When you say big money, how much you talking?"

"Five grand a game! And that's just what you see right here. There are bonuses on top of that, and the tourneys are bigger pay days. That's why this thing is international man. It's just underground right now. It's exclusive."

"Dayyumm! Five thousand dollars a game! Are you serious?"

"Yeah, and there's no catch…just make sure you win. Plus, it's all tax-free baby…to an extent."

I had to pause. Those words just didn't sound right. Maybe I'm just caught up in my emotions again. Just hear him out, it's not like I have a job that's going anywhere. It could be a good opportunity for some quick cash. There is so much I don't know. With this much money on the line, there has to be a tournament fee. Who paid it and why? I just need to hear more.

We locate some barstools and Sedrick instructs me to relax. I surf through the occupied tables and settle my eyes on one of the games due to the table more so than the players occupying it. As I visually scan and record this table into my memory banks, the cared-for felt comes into view. I see two predominately white cue balls with logos on them on the table at the same time. One with a purple diamond and the other a cowboy hat—weird.

The table consists of only red and white numbered balls compared to the rainbow version I'm accustomed to. The white balls are numbered in red and the red balls are numbered in white—what! The color of the balls took my mind to not so fond memories of bumper pool.

I watched the player that owned the cowboy hat symbol cue ball pocket a red ball, quickly gaze at his opponent, and then waited for his opponent to go. I'm immediately thrown off. What type of game is this where you pocket a ball and then have to wait for your opponent to go?

Sedrick begins whispering again. "D, I know what you're thinking. This is what makes these games great! You have to have a strategy to not only pocket your ball, but set it up so your opponent does not have an easy follow-up shot every time. It is a constant strategy after every shot. Some are clearly better than others, and it makes it that much more important to study your opponent and try and figure out any weakness you can."

I'm processing too much of this mockery of pool to share Sedrick's quiet giddy acknowledgement of this game. How did I not know that he was involved in something like this before? Sedrick wasn't one to keep secrets from his friends—at least I thought, he wouldn't keep things from his best friend. "How'd you get involved in this, Sed?"

"I am a certified hustler, man! But hey, I don't have a sponsor like these two. I'm working on it, though."

As I scan the room I can see how the focus is beginning to turn to the game we were watching. The game with "sponsors" as Sedrick says.

A voracious finger point and Sedrick quickly pulls me into the importance of this moment. "You see how Jewel has two balls left and Bentley has one?"

It is a good thing I have been watching the different players because now I clearly can identify Bentley as the player with the cowboy hat cue ball and Jewel with the diamond. I wonder if everyone's cue balls are this obvious.

"Yeah, I see it."

"This is where it gets cutthroat and the game can take a crazy turn. Jewel does this as good as anyone—that's both good and bad. So now it is Bentley's turn and he has a shot to win, but sometimes it's tough to get it in the predetermined pocket to win…"

"You have to make it in a certain pocket to win?"

"Yes, that is part of the game. A pocket is selected at the beginning, a marker is placed on it, and the competitors must make the final shot in that pocket to win the game. But listen, if Bentley misses this shot, Jewel will have the opportunity to knock his cue ball in the predetermined pocket in order to win the game."

"This is ridiculous, yo!"

"What did I tell you? There is plenty of strategy to this game." A lot of craziness it seems.

"How would you even expect me to play in a tournament with this cracked-out game you said reminds you of pool? Who came up with this mess?"

"That's a story for another day." Sedrick's verbal equivalent to hush money doesn't temper my curiosity. For now, moving on seems to be the best thing to do.

The whole hall has now focused in on the sponsored players. Bentley smoothly takes the shot and watches his seven ball carom off the side of the pocket. His ball spinning back toward him keeping it as far out of range of Jewel as he possibly could. I believe I can now tell who is sponsoring Bentley, because they look heated.

"All right, man, let's go."

"Let's go—now? I'm curious who is going to win."

"This is not for fun man! This is not just a game," Sedrick's whisper has taken a serious tone. "No matter if it's Bentley or Jewel, I don't want to see the loser's face."

"It's cool, we can go."

As we walk out the doors, I hear subdued clapping. I turn around to see the competitors briefly shaking hands. I immediately look toward the people living and dying with each shot by Bentley, and the looks on their faces told me all I needed to know. It was time to go.

Chapter 3

DUTY CALLS

I can't seem to get out of bed this morning. Falling asleep last night wasn't any better. What has Sed roped me into? Yeah, I can play pool a little bit, but I am by no means a pro. Competition fires me up. In no case can you count on greatness just because of focus. Either way, there are two things he left me with when he dropped me off: Don't talk about it, and get ready! No wonder I couldn't sleep. Right now though, I need to get ready for work and check on mom.

No one loves the feeling of a one-way game of hide-and-seek. After three minutes of it, it appears that mom is out. A ride to work would be nice; however, public transportation calls…again. Sometimes I wonder if she does this with a message in mind. She never flat out tells me to get my own place, nor should she have to. A part of me believes she still wants me here, but that same part of me doesn't see the use of a car here either. The other part empathizes with mom and views it as me being dependent.

The bus ride is quiet. It's exactly what I need and counter to my place of business on a holiday weekend. I blink, it is over with, and it was time to brace the elements. I can't wait until the warm weather greets us again. The looks on my fellow sneaker marchers' faces say they are thinking the same thing. But no matter how many times I see the smoke streaming from my nose, I wouldn't trade this place for anywhere or anything. My uncle also loved it here.

Uncle Reggie liked to tote me around like a trophy. It allowed me to see places and things I shouldn't have seen at my age. As long as I was with him, I was never worried. He would tell me our family history in this area was rich without the dollars to show for it. Uncle Reggie wanted me to be mindful of where the family has been. He likened the family to an indigenous plant that begins its journey in soil, but out of nurture and care, it blooms into something to be treasured. I never liked the reference. I always sought for something more lasting. Why do you have to wilt just to come back? If not understood, at least I still remembered it. That's all I have left of him now…memories. To carry his metaphor forward, our family needs to continue to grow. Be progressive. Sprout seeds to be planted, cultivated, and spread so we will no longer be a single sight of admiration, rather something that manifests into a timeless entity. Even the thought seems cheesy, but this is one of many lessons my uncle tried to instill in me. I want to make sure I hold on to every one of them.

As I approach work, the thoughts of last night are repressed. I need all my strength dealing with this place. The last thing I want to see when I walk in is my boss. I get it; a boss is not your friend. The issue with this gruff, senile, country strong being is that he will come across as your friend and treats you like an enemy. What kind of competent boss distributes tasks based on eye contact? I just want to avoid conta—too late for that. The chilling gaze is upon me. I'm sure his average body temperature is sub-ninety-five degrees Fahrenheit. If I didn't have to go through this employee door to clock in, I wouldn't use it at all.

"Hey, Darren, how are you? We need you in the back today; we have a truck coming in." I love how people speak to you and then don't give you a chance to respond. It makes me want to engage with them that much more. I don't get it.

"No problem, Rodrigo! As soon as I sign in, I'll head back there." The task given, on the other hand, isn't bad. It offers a temporary therapeutic reprieve. Maybe he's in a decent mood today, or I just walked in at the right time.

Truck is a blessing today. It gives me a few hours away from customers to further digest what is happening and consider if I want to go through with this whole Spikes thing. Strangely enough, with Sed's proclamation last night, I feel a sense of responsibility to see it through. Is it the competitor in me? Could it be a childish stubbornness to conquer any challenge? Or is it a distraction from dealing with the loss of Uncle Reggie? The only way to get these answers is to march on.

"Worry not about the trouble you face, rather concern yourself with your face. That is where the problem lies." Hyung belts those words like a Shakespearean groupie.

"Let me ask you one question, Hyung: why?" Hyung laughs at my suggestive comment. He does not seem to consider the reaction. He takes pride in the delivery of his material.

"You know that was a good one. Give me that—it was better than the last few at least, right?"

"How can a joke be delivered in that way and be taken seriously, Hyung? I don't think you think these things through."

"I do! It's my future Darren, just wait and see. Anyway, it's good to see you. Haven't worked with you in a while. How you holdin' up?"

Although his jokes didn't have much thought, Hyung was my favorite person to work with. He is always thoughtful and willing to put himself out there. I have seen him shut down by customers and coworkers, but he doesn't change his stripes. I always respected him for that.

"I'm doing okay. Worry about my mom and grandma. It's always hard losing a loved one."

"Tell me about it. My family is alive, but they might as well be dead. I lost them as soon as I decided to study in America. It has been worth it. The people are not very welcoming at times, but the individual freedoms make up for anything any one person can do to me. You know?"

I have spent my whole life in the United States, and Hyung feels freer than I do right now. I cannot ignore what he says. His perception is on point. Sedrick's stunt last night shouldn't get to me. There was no contract signed. I don't have to commit to it. It is just something added in my life that I do not need. I just need to put my head down and work.

"I hear ya. You seem to be doing right by yourself."

"Don't have much of a choice. I can't afford to sit around and wait for something to happen. I'm in the mindset of making it happen. You should be too! But you have to get out of your mom's house, bro. That's just not a good look."

Hyung and I remain so heavy in conversation that time is flying by. Of course, there is someone always watching.

"Every time I am over here by you two, you are doing more talking than working," Stacy says with envy and the sense of someone knowing a secret that they may or may not pass on.

"It's just a coincidence, Stacy." I am trying to keep her from lighting the kindling.

"Please, come, Stacy of HR…and partake in our celebration of employment. May any report you author speak of the glory that lies in the delivery of the package and is devoid of a trip to the gallows for us motivated commoners." I cringe as the words spew from Hyung's mouth. I don't realize what is going to be worse from the result. The fact that she isn't saying anything or the look that seems to say we are truly a waste. Hopefully, we are just a waste of time for her to deal with. No matter my situation, I can always count on a fun shift with Hyung.

* * *

I feel a heaviness slink off my body as I walk through the front door. Finally home after my shift, I can feel the good vibes coming from the kitchen. Mom is on the phone laughing, quite loud actually, and she seems to be in good spirits. Her laugh puts a smile on my face. It helps me feel like she is going to be okay. I head up to my room peacefully. I'll wait here until she's available to talk. It has been a while since mom and I have had a good talk—just her and I. I think it would be good for both of us.

As my phone vibrates I hesitate to look, but see that it is Sedrick. "Wasup, Sed?"

"You ready to change your life?"

"Stop with the drama, Sed. What'cha want, I'm busy."

"Somebody is extra spicy tonight…I don't need much. Wanted to find out if you were ready to get a lesson in, but you sound like one of the seven dwarves—pick one. It's fine, I'll call you tomorrow, but realize the tournament date is not changing."

"This is what I'm talking about, man. I didn't ask to be in this tournament. I didn't ask to take part in this game period. I just went out with you because you always look out for me. Now, look what it is turning into. This is not what I want, Sed. You were wrong about this one. First time for everything right?"

"You right. There is a first time, but not this time. I trust my instincts man. I was hesitant to introduce you to this. Haven told me this wasn't for you, and I believe him to an extent. But D, this is for you! I believe it! You are the most competitive person I know and you can do it with a smile."

The hypocrisy of his "belief" apparently escaped Sed. I hear mom wrapping up her conversation downstairs.

"I'm just not feeling it, Sed. Too many unknowns."

"It's a whole different culture, I know! But I'm telling you, D, you step away from this, you'll have regret. Don't give up on this."

I'm going to choose to ignore this pseudo threat and put a bow on this conversation.

"Sed, I'm not doing anything tonight. This feels more like pressure than you thinking about my well-being. I don't need this. I never even knew about it before last night so why would I regret it. I'm out, Sed."

"Okay, D…I'll catch up with you tomorrow."

Sed may not be in the best of spirits after that conversation, but my mom still is. Honestly, I feel a little better too.

My sense of smell becomes dominant as I take in one of my mom's great meals brewing up. Sometimes the anticipation for dinner is better than Christmas. When I get close enough to make eye contact, all I want to do is hug her.

"Okay, does this mean you are moving out?"

My head tilts back off her shoulder with my face maintaining a whatcha-talkin'-about look. There may have been a little joke involved with that statement, but it sounded like a little truth behind it as well. It's as if the English language was not hard enough to understand already. Then you throw in the nonverbals, interpretation, and don't forget to smatter in your homonyms, and it can be even harder to understand people you are closest to than anyone else.

I thought the people closest to you would be the ones that give it to you straight. Uncle Reg was great about that. He told me like it was. I know partly because when he was really going to drop some knowledge he would preface it with, "Imma tell you like it is." My mom, on the other hand, was a little harder to read.

"Are you serious, Ma?"

"Of course not, baby, but you and I both know you can't stay with me forever."

"I know, Ma, and I've saved up a good amount. As much as you don't want me here, I don't want you to have to worry about taking care of me."

"Taking care of you does not stop when you move, boy. I'm still your mama."

Like most mothers, my mom knows when to gently but firmly remind me of her place in my life. I'm lucky to have her.

The dinner was amazing—it always is when she cooks. Mom and I have a great back and forth discussion about when she would sit down with her family and watch shows in the past compared to the much more accessible world today. We should have more conversations like this, but with her schedule and my job it is hard to find time to sit down and have dinner together.

I could not let the conversation end without asking her about her phone call. A dog on a meat truck would not have been as happy as my mom was on that phone call.

"Ma, who was on the phone earlier, Aunt Terry?"

"No, it was a friend. It's always good to catch up with folks. Why you in my business anyway?"

"I'm not, Ma." The smile will not leave my face. "I just had not seen you laugh like that in a very long time. I thought I was the only one to make you laugh like that."

"You are so nosy, boy. I will tell you this. You might have a chance to meet him if things work out down the road. We are both busy people but enjoy each other's company. It would be nice to have a companion, but I'm not rushing into anything."

"I'm really happy for you, Ma, I really am. Let me know when he is coming over, and I'll be sure to hide all those action figures you have."

"They are not action figures; they are collectible figurines, and if he don't like it, he can go somewhere because those figurines aren't going anywhere!"

Her toothy smile was genuine and the sentiment was honest. Her honesty has lowered my guard even more.

"I haven't been myself lately, Ma. I feel like a part of my soul is gone."

"You were very close to my brother. I wouldn't expect anything less. My brother was not the easiest life to watch play out, but he loved you. He probably loved and valued you more than his own life. What you can't do is let his story end here. Allow it to be a starting gun versus a finish line. Do better because of it, not worse due to it. It is hard for all of us—and for varying reasons, but know he lived his life exactly how he wanted to and had no regrets.

The loss of a loved one is tough for everyone. Understand, you are a grown man and a strong one too. Keep your faith and know who is always looking over you. You will be fine. Your uncle wouldn't want you grieving over him. You know that, right? He would want you out there doing everything it took to give yourself the life you deserve. Tomorrow is not promised. But unlike him, Darren, I need you to be a bit smarter."

"Why you say that, Ma? How did Uncle Reggie die?"

"Reggie's cause of death was due to natural causes, nothing more. All I'm asking for you to do is to use that smart mind of yours, and everything will be okay."

"I will, Ma, don't worry about that. I have a lot I want to accomplish."

"I believe you. You'll be alright. Aunt Terry is always offering you work. I don't know why you won't take the job."

"I have a decent job. I don't think I need two…"

"But you still in this house." Her tone sounds a little less playful than it did before, and it didn't sound playful the last time.

"Yes, but I'm working on that."

I couldn't help but grin at that. She was right. I don't need to remain stuck in my ways.

"This was a good talk, Ma. We should open up to each other like this more."

"I'm always open! This might be new to you, but you can't live life closed off."

Her tone was vibrant and I loved it. This is what I needed. Decisions are so much easier when a loved one is in your corner.

"Okay, okay, Ma. I got you." We smile at each other as I grab our plates and start to leave the table.

"Don't think I didn't realize the only reason you wanted to talk to me was to be nosy."

"Ma, c'mon, no, it wasn't. Seriously?"

"Mm hmm, I know."

"I love you too, Ma."

I give her a kiss before I head back upstairs. I feel comfortable making my next move, and I'm not going to look back.

"Sed, can you come get me?"

Chapter 4

PLANTING SEEDS

"Every time I come here I think about how ironic the name of this place is…Bushleague Billiards. I have seen some of the Spikes elite knock around a few in here." Sedrick continues, "It's interesting to watch them murder 8-ball. I mean, these players are just talented and take the game seriously. But anyways, D, this is just to get you going. I don't expect you to be great, yet."

"Let's get started, then! My drink is finished, the marinara is gone and there are still sticks left, I'm here to play pool and we are acting like we are catching up at the bar, bro. Let's go!"

"Man…I don't know why your family thinks you're funny." Sedrick laughs. "Okay, so check it, patience is your friend. There are many strategies to this game, but we will start with the basics."

Sedrick begins a journey through the details of the game. It seems simplified. Nuanced strategy is built-in that will help each individual player insert their own measure of strategy. I am still soaking in the fact that there are two cue balls on the table. There is a competitive bite to this game that I silently feel I will enjoy. Sedrick's animation as he talks about this game is comparable to a wine bottle being uncorked in celebration. His passion is evident. The fact is it would do me some good to get invested in a hobby. The talk with my mom helped me understand that. I'm going to give my all to this tournament and roll with it. Even if I end up hating it, I can just quit and move on.

"Great shot, D! You got a lot of work ahead of you, but that's all mental. Once you get that down, I know that fire is going to carry you."

"If you got this game figured out, why aren't you sponsored?"

"Just haven't caught the right eye, I guess. Sometimes I think I should be, and then I snapback and realize I'm just glad I'm able to get some pocket change out of this. You know?"

"I'm trying to. I'm taking all this in slowly—don't want to rush it."

Sedrick just caught a glimpse of someone who walked in. His eyes are tracing his steps following from a distance.

"Darren, look over there. That's the organizer of Spikes! The unspoken protocol is that no one talks to him outside of the business arena, but man…if I just had a moment with him."

I can see the seriousness in Sedrick's face. There is a genuine affinity for this character, and if it makes him happy, I would want the chip for Sed. This is an opportunity to gauge how rational he is. One chance I'm not going to pass up.

"What would you say?"

"My ideas for the game and beyond! No matter how rich you are, people are always open to a vision that affects their pockets."

I nod. He is right about that. What he doesn't consider is the source. While I agree that people are open to this information, they are not open to it from just anyone.

"Sed, he doesn't know who you are. You need to find out his motivations. Somehow, you need to get in his crosshairs."

"Unfortunately, I don't have time for that, D. I need to make moves now. There are two ways of thinking of this: One is I can take it as a coincidence that you asked me to take you out on that same night the kingpin of the game himself would be here; The second, no matter what opportunity presents itself I must capitalize on it, because the chances of lightning striking twice in the same place are slim. Me, I'm going with the second option. There is no tomorrow, D. That's how you gotta live. Even you said your favorite uncle was always moving. I'm moving, D, I got to."

Sedrick puts his stick down and starts making his way over to the Spikes creator. I see him intercepted by someone from the entourage. As he is pulled to the side, another member talks to one of the women in the group.

I often overthink my decisions but the longer the conversation goes the more uneasy I feel. I have to give him credit for his self-belief. That is more than what I can say. One thing is for sure, if I'm doing this thing I want to get my own stick because I am tired of using these. I see Sedrick wrapping up his conversation as he begins to walk back to the table.

"So how'd it go?"

"You know how I do, how you think it went?" Sed smiles. "It went better than expected. I got a number so I can set up a meeting with the big man in the future."

"Wow! That's awesome Sed."

"Some doubt, I do! I need to get you on my level, so let's refocus."

I'm happy for Sed. He needs a win. I prepare my shot but before I do, I take a look in the direction of the group. The woman that was talking to Sed and the creator are in full eye contact lock mode on me!

"Sed, don't look, but the woman you were just talking to is with the Spikes creator, and they are looking over here."

Sedrick doesn't listen and immediately looks over there. His wave goes unreturned, and then they both look away and rejoin the rest of their group.

"I told you not to look!"

"It was just another opportunity to me; it's just that one didn't go as well."

"It looked like they were looking right at me, man."

"That's because you can be a little into yourself sometimes."

"Huh?"

"You heard me, you are not vain, but you think things are about you more than they really are."

Sed pockets a ball trying to subtly get his dig in and move on, but I'm not that easy.

"I'm one of the most selfless people I'm aware of."

"Annnd how many times has someone else said that about you?"

I miss two easy shots while Sed pockets two more balls.

"I can't just remember a conversation out of the blue that my selflessness came up. That seems a little self-serving to even think about."

"Well, I can remember when a girl would say hi to you, it was a confession of love. Oh, and I can remember when a scout that was not at the game for you told you, you had a nice shot, you thought you should be in the league. Shall I continue…?"

"The things you remember, and yet I'll be buried before you remember a birthday."

"We ain't married, bro!"

We continue the back and forth until Sed pockets his last ball.

"You see, D; this is what you need to work on. I played two mental games and both played with your emotions. First, you got upset because I called you selfish. Then I reined it in with a smile providing you reassurance that this was all in fun and we are still cool…"

Hearing Sedrick talk like this made me wonder what is real and what isn't. Maybe he is right. I continue to claim things that are not true. The contradictions I have in life are highly prevalent and if he can point them out this easy I can't imagine what my family thinks.

"D, it's cool, seriously. I've been played before. You can't do that in this game. Once you fall a ball behind, it is incredibly hard to come back. The high-level players are that good. The mental game is important."

"I hear you, but Sed, the other night when we were watching those players. You know…the ones that were sponsored. You could hear a pin drop in there. There was no talking, there were no jabs going back and forth. They were very business-like. I can't tell if this is like golf or is it like a team sport."

"Tourney play is more intense along with players with history. Jewel and Bentley have history. The good news is that they have a lot of respect for one another. That's not the case all the time. As a matter of fact, I would say it is fifty-fifty when it comes to the belligerent folks compared to others. The game is constantly evolving. The only thing that is asked is that the crowd takes on the competitor's spirit. That just means, don't be obnoxious and cheer loud if they are not bothered. I like the rowdy crowds personally."

"Sed, you know a lot about this game. You brought me into this and I might not hate you for it down the line, but I feel like we have talked so much about this game. What's up with you, bro? How have things really been? You never even told me about you and Briana"

"Oh, you trying to get in my head now, huh?"

"No games, Sed; I'm serious."

"I know, fool, I'm just playing, dang… Okay, well, me and Briana are cool. We still vibe and things are good between us. We are not getting married anytime soon or nothing, but I'm still at her place and we are just, you know, taking our time with things."

"What does she think about Spikes? Did you put her through your boot camp?"

"She doesn't know…and I won't tell her. And you won't tell her."

"Okay, Sed! I didn't know it was like that. I understand. It's an underground game. You probably don't wan—"

"That's not it! Look, I'm trying to pull you in on something that's got nice money involved and eventually, who knows, you could be a coveted star of this thing. But the fact is, Briana doesn't need to know what I'm doing, how I'm doing it, and the reason I do things. I'm married to this game, not her…well, at least at the moment. I'm like a promoter and talent agent. I just know talent, even if I only have a little to speak of."

"You shouldn't doubt yourself, Sed. No one can talk a game like you, and you seem pretty good to me."

Sed looks at me and slowly puts his stick down. His face reeks of agitation as he begins walking to my side of the table.

"Let's pick this up another time."

"Something I said, huh?"

"Yeah, but it's cool, I'm good…we're good. The appetite just faded."

Sedrick pulls up to my mom's house with what was a borderline uncomfortable quiet ride home. I hit a nerve with something I said, but I can't make out if it was me bringing up Briana or something else. I'll just give him his time. It's been a busy last few days and a whirlwind of things going on. Maybe we both need to get our thoughts together before we link up again.

Chapter 5

WORKERS' COMPENSATION

The day advocates that the sun's copious rays shine bright on one of the tallest buildings in the city. Perhaps this is nature's way to highlight the beauty of this architectural marvel or serve as a spotlight to warn others of the peculiarity within it.

"Mr. Bryant?"

"Yes!"

"Mr. Finney will see you now."

"Thank you."

Sedrick takes one last look at the uncomfortable furniture. Understandably, sitting on egg shells for fear of breaking them would be disconcerting.

"Hey, Sedrick, good to see you…close the door please." Mr. Finney chokes out the natural light. Simultaneously, the room's lighting adjusts accordingly.

"Mr. Finney, I want to thank you for the opportunity and apologize for—"

"*Stop*! You made a poor choice a couple of nights ago, but by the look of you, that was just one of many. The terms of engagement are clear."

"Yes, sir, I understand. I just wanted to let you know that I have a plan."

"Sedrick, listen to yourself and then take a look around. How do you think I was able to sit in the big chair? How do you think I was able to successfully balance a multibillion-dollar corporation and the most successful, international, and might I add, lucrative games of billiards ever? Do you have an idea?"

"It's because you worked hard and achieved it."

Laughter from Mr. Finney fills the room.

"Hard work is subjective Sedrick. It's not about hard work. Let's go back to your initial words. You said you had a plan. A plan is something that requires an initial thought of an idea that manifests itself into goals, objectives, and achievements which culminate into the 'plan' being fulfilled. But that's not where it ends. Plans have branches. If the plan is big enough, it doesn't end. It constantly evolves and morphs into something that either you are able to keep up with and stay ahead of or something that needs to be inherited by someone capable of taking on the responsibility. Not all plans are created equal. I had a plan that metastasized into what you see, feel, touch, and wish you could revel in. All plans...no matter the size will hit a proverbial crossroads. Is that where your plan is?"

"No crossroads, yet. As I stated the other night, I have a plan to get your money back, and you got your first look at him at Bushleague's," Sedrick states with a shaky confidence.

"Sedrick, come on," Mr. Finney smiles. "You are a prototypical hustler, and I love that about you. I am a hustler as well. I can see a future where you could be an integral part of the expansion of our game. Heck, maybe you can help lead us to legitimacy one day. You have a ways to go before you get there. But I can't trust you, Sedrick. It's like a plan. Sometimes you just need to know when to cut your losses and go back to the drawing board. There is one thing you need to know about me...I can't be played, Sedrick. Okay, so speed this up, I have a meeting shortly, so tell me your plan."

"You're not going to believe this..." Sedrick's eyes widen as he spews out news for Finney.

"Try me."

"The guy you were looking at the other night is the nephew of Reggie Stokes."

"Fireball?"

"Yeah... Fireball."

"Wow, that's interesting—Sorry to hear about his passing. Fireball was a phenomenal player. His ego got the best of him, but other than that, he was dang near untouchable."

"I know, and so is his nephew. He must have been secretly teaching him. I caught wind of it since I'm a friend of the family."

"Wait, so you found another member of that family to take the fall for you, Sedrick! I'm impressed. Seriously, how do you do it? It was crazy enough that Fireball took on your debts to get you out of trouble. I remember when he came to me. Confident. Secure. Not a doubt in the world he would win enough money to pay off your debt while conquering his own vices. The game is a gamble, and sometimes when you gamble on yourself too much, you lose. It is sad to watch someone so talented be swallowed up by the very thing they loved to consume. It is like watching a lion go after their prey in the Serengeti. It's savage! There's nothing you can do, but a part of you watches in amazement. Then you move on with your life. It's a vulnerable moment that can remind you how weak some are and how strong others can be. It is a primal world; I just don't think the savage part of life should be public. Paints a messy image. But anyways, back on track…my money, your plan?"

"He will play in the tournament. He will win. You will get your money. My only thing is, once he wins, you hire me. I don't care if it's under the table or not. I want to be part of the staff. Listen, I know this game up and down. I'm just not the best at playing it. I can spot talent and most importantly the personalities that fit this type of game. I want to be that guy for you. If you see me fitting in somewhere else, then, I'll see if I'm interested."

Mr. Finney nods in approval.

"It's funny, you owe me money and now you ask me for a job before you pay me back." Finney laughs. "I like you, Sedrick, and I accept these terms. I do think you would be an asset to my team. I need you to understand a few things here. First, I don't want to see your face in this office again. Second, if you see me out, you ignore me. Third, the stakes are raised, this is a major tournament and a big risk to put anyone in, no matter if it's Fireball's nephew. I agree to your terms, your friend wins this, you are clear. I will tell you, if he doesn't win…may God bless you both. I hope he understands these stakes."

"He understands the risk. We're good. The only thing I need to know is, after the tournament, when do I start?" Sedrick winks.

"If your boy wins, welcome to the team. I'll find you. If he doesn't, at least it was a good run in this game, right? Get out Sedrick."

* * *

Finally, I see Sedrick heading this way after his meeting.

"You were up there for a while."

"That's how it is when you have so many ideas. I had to get them all out there."

"So how did it go?"

"Let's get to the car first."

For Sedrick's sake, I hope this meeting went well. He could use some good news. As much as he has been looking out for my well-being after losing my uncle, it would be nice to hear something positive happening for him. As we settle into the car, I wait for him to break the silence.

"I can't tell you how excited I am, D!" Sedrick's tone is of happiness. The meeting must have gone well for him.

"So, it went that well! That's good! Let's go get something to eat, I'm buying."

"I'm down…so, check this out. This man liked my ideas so much he offered me a job!"

"A job! That's awesome, Sed! Did you accept?"

"Of course, I took it, but he told me the position will not be available until after that major tournament that is coming up. There is some time and some lower-level games we can get into. I'll make sure you are ready to go, don't worry."

"Wait, Sed, is this a job working underground or legitimate?"

"It doesn't matter man. He is legit, and either way, I get major paid!"

"Listen, Sed, I'm happy for you getting a job, but don't you want to go legit? You don't pay taxes on this. How can you show proof of income and still be bringing home bank? You'll be investigated in no time."

"See, D, guys like you sometimes lack that vision. Bro, he has positions posing from within his company to pay the people that work for him in the underground. It looks legit. I will show up when necessary for some hack jobs for some hack reason at a time he will specify, and it will be all good. There are a lot of folks on the payroll. That has helped the game thrive. He's got it under control and so do I. I would just be assigned to different position, higher paygrade, if you know what I'm sayin'."

"I just don't want you to get caught up."

"I got this, D, don't worry. This is finally gonna be my break. We just need to get you on a level to win this tournament."

As we pull up to the restaurant, I still have my concerns about his proposition. Sedrick is always grinding, but sometimes a leap of faith can be viewed as attempted suicide through the eyes of the less optimistic.

"After we're done, Sed, I need you to drop me off at the house. I'm having dinner with my mom and her new man. I'm trying to be open to this since my mom won't just bring anyone to the house, and she wants me to meet the guy."

"Whoa, okay, okay. Mama Stokes is serious about this one. Make sure you check him for weapons and condoms, man. You can't have none of that business going down when you're home," Sedrick laughs.

"What is wrong with you, Sed?" Darren shakes his head. "I'm not going to freak the man out."

"Do you know anything about him?"

"Not too much, but I'll be sure to interrogate him and report back to you, Director."

"See, now that's what I'm talking about. I'm attracted to crazy so no one knows it like I do."

"So that's why you haven't proposed to Briana yet."

"You bring up Briana all the time, it's like you want to be with her."

"I would never date her after you, but I'm not going to lie, I think she is my type."

"Oh that's right, she did say hi to you once, I get it," Sedrick smiles and looks at the clock.

"You gotta roll?"

"Yeah, I better get goin' and get you back to the house so you can setup the cameras," Sedrick expresses a cheesy grin. "Hey, you available after dinner tonight?"

"No, I'm going to be busy with work for the next couple weeks. I have some extra shifts I'm working and trying to spend some more time with my mom. I need to save man. I'm trying to move out."

"Well, it's about damn time! Okay, if you have some time at least work on some of the things we went over. Oh, and take this."

"What is it?"

"It's the rules of the game. I put them on paper to help you understand the basics. In about a couple weeks, there is a little something going on at the spot. I want you to be there. Maybe you can get a small stakes game or two in."

"Do you think I can get one in without money first?"

"Only if it's just me and you. But yeah, we can work it in."

"I'll be there, but we will need to work in a game or two, just us before that at Bushleague's or something."

"My man…no problem. Alright man, let's go. I want to make sure I get you home so you can meet your new daddy."

"Ha ha, funny, Sed. Hey, make sure you let Briana know I had fun too."

"Eh, okay, okay, I'll give it to you. That one was actually half decent."

"I wasn't joking."

As I exit the car and head toward the house, I can sense my smile only getting bigger. This is probably the best feeling I have had since Uncle Reg passed. I don't know what this new guy has to offer my mom, but he is lucky I am in a good mood today.

Chapter 6

AN EXTRA TABLE SETTING

I didn't think my mood could change. I walked by the living room and snuck a quick look at my mom to see her smile begin to fade as the clock continues to tick with no one knocking at the door. She was able to get off work early today. She came home and prepared one of her staples while still making time to prepare herself for the evening. She is ever so thoughtful and respectful of people's time! I can tell this is an important night for her.

"You look great, Ma."

"Thank you. And thank you for being here for this. It means a lot to me."

"Anything for you, Ma. Apparently our guest is missing one of these," I point to my watch feeling a little edgy, but also not wanting to make my mother feel worse than she already does.

"Let's give him a chance. This is his first time here and navigating the spaghetti bowl to take that quick exit takes some time to get used to."

"C'mon, Ma, you're not making excuses for him now, are you?"

"I'm serious! A good judge doesn't make a decision without the facts, so watch yourself." My mom had a way of teaching me mini lessons in any setting. It always made sense. Whether I agreed or disagreed was not important. The message was what was important. I heard her loud and clear.

Finally, a knock at the door.

"Hey!"

My mom immediately reaches in and provides a hug. My heart sinks a little at the sight of this. There is a tiny pain as if something is being stripped from my heart. Thoughts are displaced as I'm suddenly in immediate discomfort. It takes some emergency mental judo to try and pull myself back in the moment.

"Brit, I am so sorry I didn't get here earlier. That spaghetti bowl was a little different to navigate."

I didn't have to look. I could feel my mom's eyes cutting in my direction after that comment. Affirmation is a wonderful thing when you are on the winning side.

"Darren and I were just talking about how that is probably what happened. No apology needed. We *both* understand how crazy the bowl is. Right, baby?"

"Absolutely! I'm surprised you made it when you did. You are right on time!"

A fake smile can't hide the coating of sarcasm brimming from that comment. I'll take the squinty eye I received back as a sign of acknowledgement and disapproval. Time for me to scale back. This is her night. I need to be there for her and not against her, even though he shouldn't have been late to begin with. Spaghetti bowl or not, it's not his first time driving in this city.

"Yeah, this is my first time driving on this side of the city. Normally, I take the train or a bus, but I didn't want to take any chances of missing dinner," Myron humbly states.

Is this guy serious? He is laying it on way too thick early on. He knows I'm here and watching. Maybe that was a play to let me know he was here to stay. He needs to understand, so am I.

"Myron, this is my son, Darren."

"How you doing, Darren?"

"Pretty hungry, but besides that I am doing well. I'm happy to finally meet you. My mom has mentioned you on many occasions."

"That's a good thing, I hope."

"It's a mixed bag, which is why I'm here tonight."

"Oh really…" I can see the wonder in Myron's eyes.

"Darren…uh uh," a slow and forceful shake of the head put me on notice.

It was time for me to shut down the onslaught. My mom just tied the "hard to get son" ploy to the docks. It's time to let another boat sail.

"All right, Ma, all right. I will go get us all drinks."

"Thanks. I'll have a rum and Coke," Myron spouts. "Your mom would like the same."

"No, Myron, not now," Brittany presents a blushing giggle.

As Myron smiles, his eyes meet mine. I can tell he thinks he got the last laugh with his implication of future inebriation and possible extracurricular activity. I am not going to let this man shake me. I will just get them both tea and stir his with my finger. No, stop it. Grow up. My mom loves this guy. I have to give him a chance no matter what his sinful eyes try to convince me of.

Dinner is going well. It feels so good to see my mom smile. He is a good talker. I like how he doesn't focus on himself at all. Everything is about my mom. She needs that. She needs someone in her life that will be devoted to her. I can sense it really is time for me to find my own place as soon as possible. With how smooth everything has been going, there are a few things I forgot to ask. Dinner was just so good!

"Myron, what do you do?"

"I'm a behavioral psychiatrist. I work at the Rever Medical Clinic but most of my clients are elsewhere. I don't like to talk about it. Comes off as me being pretentious. And that's not me." His smile says otherwise. "Are you interested in pursuing the medical field? It's not too late."

"Sounds like you are doing some assuming…like I don't have a path or I don't have my education already."

"I didn't mean it like that. Me and your mom talk, so I ha—"

"What are you saying about me, Ma?"

My mom's face is now uncomfortable. I need to tread lightly here, but I don't want my name coming out of someone's mouth that thinks they know me, just because they heard from someone else. Oh wow…I should listen to myself. This is exactly what my mom was trying tell me. Not to judge before thoroughly knowing the facts.

"I'm not saying anything negative, Darren," my mom states empathetically.

"Please allow me to restate, what do you want to do Darren? Do you want to continue to work at the warehouse and move up the chain there or are you in pursuit of another career path?"

Although I cringed that he knew where I worked, I am going to grit my teeth and move on.

"I have some options out there; I just haven't decided which way I'm headed yet."

"It's important that you take your time and explore your options. At least by then, when you commit to it, you will know that is your path. I wish I could say the same about my job. I wanted this job strictly for the money and what that money could do for me. The title of 'doctor' in front of my name and any bit of prestige that comes with that, I wanted. Once I got into it, I was humbled. I have treated many individuals with schizophrenia, bipolar disorder, attention-deficit hyperactivity disorder, and others. I saw the look in not only their eyes, but also their parents' eyes. It is a scary look. If you can ever think of a time when you tried everything you could to figure out a problem or an issue and still couldn't figure it out…when you are almost to the breaking point of quitting or giving up. That is the look I see in the parents of some of my new patients.

Let me tell you…none of them want to give up, but you can see the wear and tear that it is taking. It opened my heart more than ever as time went on. I became sensitized. I didn't want to be closed off. I wanted to feel as much as I could. Don't get me wrong. It takes a toll each and every day, but it feels so rewarding when even one of my patients shows improvement from one visit to the next and to the next. All I'm saying is you need to find job fulfillment…happiness. When you find something that gives you bliss, no matter what it is, stick with it and enjoy the ride."

Not many people like to get lectured and that includes me. However, Myron was right about one thing. I need to find something that I enjoy and hold on to it. As Sedrick said, I love competition. I like working with Hyung at the warehouse, but that's not what I want to do long term.

39

"Was that your speech for your next guest speaker appearance? If so, you're going to kill it!"

I'm glad to see the smile on my mom's face; I could see she was worried where I was going with that.

"Does anyone want any dessert? I made Darren's favorite, Oreo cheesecake, and I don't brag but if you don't eat any…shame on you."

"She's not joking, Myron. I have *never* had a cheesecake that good, anywhere."

"I would love to have some, Brit, thank you."

This guy's not so bad. I don't know all the facts so I won't judge, but so far, Myron is alright.

Chapter 7

MAKE YOUR NAME

I haven't been nervous like this before. Thinking of getting my first real taste of action tonight has got me on edge. Psyching myself out is not working. I need to just chill and think of just murdering whoever my opponent is. I need to find that fire. What if I don't have it? What if this isn't for me after all? Those practice rounds with Sed were not stellar, but I did take it to him a couple times. No sweat, I got this. Sed will be here soon, and it will be time.

"How you feeling?" Whenever Sedrick would ask this question it meant he already had a pretty good idea of my state of mind. There are times I let him peek into my cavernous thoughts, but this time I prefer to keep them in a straightjacket.

"I feel right, Sed, but I just need to get out there and see what happens. So how is this going to work?"

"Don't worry about it, no pressure, I have already arranged it. You will be going against Camila. A solid player that has her ups and downs. She doesn't play head games, but they call her 'Spades' for a reason. I just don't know that reason yet. If she wins the lag, she never breaks. My advice to you is to force her to break…so you need to win the lag…"

"No pressure, huh." Sed's part scouting report and part pep talk is not starting well.

"Well, of course there is pressure. This is for money man! The good thing is, these tune ups can range from a few hundred dollars to

J. R. KNOX

five or ten grand. It just depends on the matchup. The bigger you get in this game the more people want to see you and the more money that will be wagered—which means, the more money in your pocket. This is an off-schedule game so it will only be a couple hundred bucks on the table. We were lucky to get a player of Spades' caliber for this, so be thankful."

"You should have just had me go against Haven."

"Hey, I'm trying to have you step out the sauna onto hot coals, not jump in the volcano."

"None of those sound appealing."

"That's the game, D. Doubt is your worse enemy. You have it in you, I have seen it. I can't wait to see it come back." Finally, something I can use. Diffuse the doubt in my mind. It is draining.

Sedrick walks in first as we head to the Spikes room. I didn't want to shake hands with anyone with my unrelentingly clammy hands. Subtle fist bumps will have to do. Sedrick sits with Tory and Haven and I can't keep myself from scanning the room. I search for something to hold on to in order to calm these nerves.

"Here." A random stranger offers me a drink.

"Thanks, but I'm not drinking tonight." My response is filled with purpose and strength. I'm sure it comes across as a façade. Any of these players see a weakness; I know I'll look like fresh meat in a lion's den. I need to get in my zone.

"So are you Sedrick's protégé?" Her words caused me to refocus on her. Where did she hear that from?

"I'm just here to play. I'm no one's protégé. Is Sed helping me out? Yes! This is a solo game, and I have my own motivations." I don't think I could have lied any better than this giving my current volatile state.

"Okay, Mr. Motivations, my name is Suds." She extends her hand for a standard greeting but everyone is getting a fist bump until my hands dry out. It seems like she has some manners about her. "No, that's not my real name, just wanted to wish you luck tonight. I like to start my night out with one of these. It relaxes me. Some people think I'm an alcoholic, but to be honest"—why is she leaning in so close?—"the only time I drink is before a game or match. That doesn't stop them from calling me Suds. You can imagine what my cue ball looks like right? I'm pretty laid back when I'm not playing so if there is something you need to know, let me know."

"What are you doing, Suds? Away from my man. He's getting ready to show out." Sedrick just came out of nowhere to interrupt our conversation.

"Calm down, Boomerang. It's good for him to get some advice from someone with some actual talent."

"Take your drunk self home; you don't play for another hour. What is that, your third or fourth drink to *calm your nerves?*"

She calmly let Sedrick know he was number one and walked away. To say there was animosity between them would be polite. She also called Sed by a tag or a nickname, Boomerang. I didn't think he was sponsored.

"I don't need you to come protect me, Sed. I was just fine."

"You remember how I said it is fifty-fifty with people talking and not talking while they play. She is on the side that talks. I don't know how she plays as well as she does with as much as she drinks."

I look over at Suds, and she was gleefully laughing and joking with another group of people I didn't know. She obviously didn't let Sedrick get to her. I needed to ask Sed about this Boomerang name.

"So Boomerang, what's next? I thought you weren't sponsored."

Sedrick looks at me with a petulant smile. "It's because I have a knack for coming back. I don't like to talk about it. Feels like I'm not sponsored with the way I'm treated. Anyways, don't worry, by the time the tournament comes around you will have a personalized cue too."

"That sounds like you are hardly ahead—maybe that has to do with your *treatment.*"

"Speak what you know, pahtna. And you don't know this. Let's just get this game going. You can't talk until you make a name for yourself."

There are quite a few games going on today. More than the last time I was here. The sidewalls are concealed by the wallpaper of cloth and flesh. I can't decipher spectator from sponsor. There is a notable gathering of them huddled close to a playing table in the back corner that has only one contestant. She is standing there waiting and now she is looking at Sed. Suds provides a brief greeting to the stoic competitor and now is heading our way.

"Drew a crowd for your first game, I see! Good luck going against Camila, oh wait…Spades. Lesson one, always use the tag name. When facing Spades, the only thing guaranteed is boredom. Doesn't talk much…"

"Suds, really? Away from him, away now, dang."

"So possessive, Sedrick…well, good luck and shoot straight. A lot of curious eyes on you today."

"Thanks, Suds. I'll try not to disappoint. Luckily, I'm known to lock in when it's time—unfortunately, I'm noticing everything right now!"

Sedrick gently shoves Suds away and she waves goodbye.

"You need to be punctual to these things, man. Let's go, no more distractions."

"Okay, okay."

Sedrick begins talking to what looks like an official, and wow, they look sharp. Spades has made minimal eye contact with me since I have been at the table. My hands are finally drying out which is a good sign and at a perfect time to properly introduce myself and see what I can discover.

"Hey, I'm Darren."

I slowly start to pull back my hands as this seems to be going sour. Then she reached out.

"Spades…first time?"

"Yes."

"From what I hear and the look of the people around here, you must be someone special." Even Spades is saying this. I must be the only one that is too new to notice.

"I don't know any of these people, so I don't know why they would think that."

"Who you know is less important than what you can provide. And you obviously have something to attract this attention."

"I have a will to win, that's it."

"I'd rather have skill than will in this game." Her corny but effective drop the mic comment soaks into my core paralyzing me for a second before I can get any words out. Realizing that Spades is actually talking made me more curious about her. That is not the impression others seem to have. The sting from her comment is gone and the desire to learn more about her increased.

"Hey, Spades—" Sedrick cuts me off before I can continue. I guess I will have to wait for another time.

"All right, Darren, it's time."

Spades breaks out her cue, and it is stunning. It is a multicol-ored rainbow-like cue with a larger spade on the bottom with what appears to be her initials inside of them. It has a ribbon that wraps around to the tip, lined with a gold trim that follows the ribbon that includes the shape of diamonds embedded along the route to the tip. Her cue ball has a traditional spades emblem with what looks like a silhouette of a woman shooting pool in the middle of it.

My cue isn't nearly as fancy. As a matter of fact, it is not fancy at all.

"How do I get one of those, Sed?"

"Just win and everything takes care of itself. Go get your instruc-tions from the ref, and then it's show time, baby."

The official is running through the instructions in what seems like auctioneer fashion.

"Could you repeat those, please?"

You could smell the judgement. Rehashing my mom's comment wouldn't go well here know matter how right it is. Camila shook her head, but at least she was smiling. Maybe I was easy prey for her. I could make out the questioning whispers from the gallery. Their whispers were as quiet as wind chimes in a storm.

The official begrudgingly explains the rules again, and now we are settling in for the lag. Camila has a delicate look about her, but I can sense her toughness. She looks at me and I expect her to spew a few words my way—nothing. I feel the need to say something.

"Good luck!"

She refuses to respond and readies her shot. We both have solid strikes on the lag but my lag was closer providing me the option to break or go ball in hand after my opponent breaks. I remember Sedrick telling me to let her break so I do just that.

"Ball in hand." I said it with confidence, and Sedrick nods in approval.

Camila looks at Sedrick and then me and gets in position. Her glove has an expression on it but I can't make out what it says. It looks to be in Spanish.

Her break is average at best with no balls going in, and I see a chance to knock in two red balls if played correctly right away. I take control of the first red ball by knocking it in confidently. Camila returns the favor with her white ball. The setup is as I anticipated for my second red ball. I know I didn't have much of a shot once I knock in my second ball, so I decide to take a chance and let Camila know I mean business. I manage to pocket my second red ball, and in the process, have my cue ball carom into one of her white balls giving her a more difficult opportunity. She jumps my ball and then proceeds to knock in her ball in the corner pocket. Sedrick seemed to have left out the fact that players were allowed to do that.

"Great shot."

Silence. She doesn't say a thing. She only wants to continue the onslaught.

I struggle on my next few shots. She has now pocketed four balls in a row. She just misses on one of her shots, leaving her two balls left. I'm getting my butt whipped here! I look around the room, and they are all shaking their heads as if I am not someone they thought I was—as if I was a failure. And now I'm starting to get that feeling—an extreme focus. The people are dissipating around me. My opponent, myself, and the game are the center of my focus. I begin dissecting the table and immediately see how I can end this with five strikes and solid ball placement.

I knock in my next shot and put Camila in a bad predicament with the lay. After a couple well-placed shots, I am back in the game—two left. I unlock for a brief moment and make wrathful eye contact with one of the wallflowers. I immediately lock back in. I knock down the sixth, setting up a good shot. I provide a death stare to my opponent and then I suddenly unlock. An emotion comes over me as I look at the eyes of Camila. I can see the doubt. She can see my determination. She can feel that she could lose, but there's something behind her gaze. This means something more to her. Will she be hurt if I win? The look has me worried, but I shake it off as I hear Sedrick in the background.

"That's what I'm talking about. That's what I remember."

She makes her next shot and I miss mine uncharacteristically bad. I can't hide how upset I am. Onlookers observe me like an exhibit without bars that separate them from me. Perhaps my reaction was justified.

Camila now has a chance to use her spades cue ball and knock in my currently symbol-less cue ball since she has two or less balls on the table. If she misses, she loses a turn and that is pretty much a guaranteed victory for me. It would be a difficult shot off the bank but definitely one she can hit given what I have seen so far.

She goes for her ball instead, making her shot but failing to block mine. This leaves a chip in shot for me to take the win.

It's over!

"Good game, D! You are going to light this place on fire. Camila is a solid player, and you took it to her dude."

Suds was partly right, Spades doesn't talk during the game, but she is not boring at all. I'm too nosy not to know more. I need to ask her a question.

"Thanks, Sed." I need to shake Sedrick first. "I'll be back; I'm going to talk to Spades real fast."

"That's fine, but wait until her sponsor is done with her. Speaking of sponsors, I know for sure you will have one soon. I have a tournament lined up for you. It will get you ready for the big one. Tournaments are a grind, but I know you can get through it. It's the best two out of three each round. I'm hearing they may go best three out of five for the big one though."

Sedrick blabs on while I'm focusing on Camila. As soon as I see her breaking away, I'm going to approach her.

"Camila!" I finally dart away from Sedrick.

"Good game, Darren. You have some skill to go with that will after all."

An unforced smile takes over my face. I'm happy to see she can still smile after the competition as well.

"Oh…yeah, thanks! Good game to you too…but look, um, I have a question. I know you could have taken a shot to knock my symbol cue ball in and win the game. Why didn't you?"

"Well, Darren, I have a question for you. You were in a groove and could have finished the game off by setting me up for a difficult shot a turn before that. It would have been difficult for me to counter. Why didn't you?"

"I don't know what happened. I got a little distracted."

"Exactly! I am not a charity case. I don't need you to miss shots so I can win."

"Camila, no…that wasn't it at all."

"I let you have this low stakes dog-and-pony show. It will only help you grow and help our pockets when I see you down the road. You don't realize there is a game within the game. Only a few have to play it. I'm one of those few."

Camila packs up her cue and symbol ball and walks out of the room. I didn't expect my first win to feel like this.

Chapter 8

OUTSIDE THE ARENA

As the weeks go by, I just can't get Camila out of my head. I don't see her in any billiard halls and every trip back to the scene of my first win comes up empty. I have been fortunate to beat a few competitors since then, but they were not on the level of Camila. They were not sponsored like Camila. The first of anything can hang over you and be memorable, but my thoughts are not because it was my first win. Camila was too good to not risk that shot. Once again, I must shove this memory to the background and think about today.

"Ma, so when is Myron coming over again?"

"He stopped by yesterday for a bit, but you were at work. Myron and I are having dinner tonight at his place. He wants to try to play chef."

My mom is one of the best chefs in this region so he doesn't have a shot to cook as well as her.

"Oh Lord, Ma! My advice to you is to just choke down whatever he makes, because you already know you would have done it better."

"Thanks for the advice Dr. Love. This isn't the first time Myron has cooked for me, and his cooking is pretty good. He made some smoked brisket last time—that he started smoking at two in the morning! He put some love in that meat. Mm, mm *mmm*!" I don't like that visual.

"Okay, Ma. I got it. The man can cook. Soo, I'm going to meet Sedrick in a few, but I'll be back later. And I have enough saved up for first and last month's rent, so I'm going to start looking for places. Can you keep an ear and eye out for anything?"

"I sure can. I'm proud of you, Darren, and your Uncle Reg would be proud of you too. Just know, you stay as long as you need to. I don't want you being a boomerang son!"

"What is that, Ma?"

"Those kids that you kick out of the house and a couple months or even a year later, they come right back."

"Haha, I don't plan to be one of those."

"That's why I'd rather you stay a couple extra months here than leave too early just to get out on your own."

"Thanks, Ma! I love you, and I'm on a mission. I'll get out of this house and not let up. Just watch me."

"Whatever you do, do it with a good heart. That's all I ask."

"I will, Ma."

Things have never been better between my mom and me. Maybe I should have said I was moving out earlier! I'm looking forward to heading crosstown today. I finally get to challenge Haven in a friendly game of Spikes. It will be good to go against someone of his skill level. Haven has won his fair share of tournaments and individual competitions. I'll have to ask if he will be in the final tournament before the big one.

A brisk chill feels good on a night like tonight. I can actually hear my thoughts as I walk down the street. This is a nice change. If the subway is as kind to me, I just might go buy a lottery ticket.

Being aboard this train gives me time to think about my strategy with Haven. Do I want to talk a little trash with him? Should I break or go ball in hand? Should I play it close enough and then just bury his symbol cue ball just because I can? If anything, I have realized over the last couple weeks is that I am a quick study in this game. It is becoming like a chessboard. If only the thought of strategy took me far enough away from the funk on this train though. I need to move to another car.

That's better. While entering the car, I begin to take inventory. Scanning farther down the car, I see her! It's Camila! And alone? I can't pass this up. I have to rid my mind of this hold she has had on me since we played. Subtle is the best approach, regardless of the nervous excitement inside.

"Hi, Camila."

"Hey." I was hoping for a smile, but I did just beat her in a competition…for money! I can't say I blame her for being a little apprehensive.

"I know this sounds crazy, but ever since our game I haven't been able to get you out of my mind. No matter what I do, I keep circling back to that day." That was better in my head than when it came out.

"You're wrong." She turns and looks at me. "That doesn't sound crazy; it sounds creepy." I deserve that I guess.

"I don't mean I was thinking of you in a sexual or self-fulfilling way…well maybe self-fulfilling, but what I'm trying to say is, I have to know why you did what you did."

"Why do you care? You won! That's the goal of the game. To win! I tried to win, I took the shots I needed to, to win, and I lost."

Her tone encourages me to walk away or change the topic. This might not have been a good idea. I don't know when I'll get this opportunity again. There is something I'm missing here. I feel it. Why is she riding the subway? I have made twice as much in the last week than I would by working two weeks at my job and these are small time games. If there is as much money in this as Sedrick says, why is she riding the subway? It can't hurt to ask that.

"I don't know why, but I always thought sponsored players had money. When I saw Jewel and Bentley…"

"Well, I'm not Jewel or Bentley! Look…what do you want? I'm trapped on this train, and you want to take the opportunity to torture me with probing questions? For what? Winning wasn't enough for you?"

I guess it can hurt a little. Looking at these faces taking notice of us doesn't help either. I don't even know Camila, but I am responsible for putting her in this situation. I need to recover and get to the point.

"Camila, I'm sorry. I didn't mean to offend. I just wanted to know more about the game within the game you spoke of. What did you mean?"

The fact that she has paused before responding gives me hope that I won't be emotionally beheaded. Her face softens and I can sense her transition of thought.

"People like you see the fancy arrangements. You see the people, the decorative cues, and ambience. There are a lot of players that are doing really well playing this game. I worked my butt off to get to where I am. Taking that 'L' to you set me back, but it only set me back temporarily because of what I told you. I heard all the whispers about this talented player that was trained by a legend in this game. Heard he was coming to join the party. I knew I could use you to my advantage, so I wanted first dibs as a sponsored player while a few others didn't want to take the chance. I knew I could beat you when you missed your third shot. It wasn't technique or ability that was missing. It was the will you talked about that you had. I thought you were all talk, and then I saw your eyes. When I missed, you flipped. You were possessed! At that moment, I saw what I heard all the talk was about, and then you snapped out of it. You looked me right in the eye, and I didn't like what I saw. You looked at me with pity. You looked at me as if you didn't want to embarrass me. That is what will not only get you beat Darren, but depending on the stakes, in this game, it will get you killed!"

"I'm sorry, Camila…in that moment…I, I just haven't felt that feeling in a long time. I am ultra-competitive and I have no problem beating the brakes off of a man or a woman if it's a fair competition. You're right, I did freeze. Over the last couple weeks, I have found my balance. Right now, I'm locked in, Spades—"

"Don't you call me that outside of the game! You hear me… ever!"

"Okay, okay, I won't. Just believe me when I tell you, if we played again, it would be a different game."

"You think you can play a couple weeks and you are elite! *If* we play again, I already know it will be different. I just hope you are ready. Your half-hearted apology—that sounded more self-boastful than an apology, by the way—was not necessary, but I'll accept it. I hope you know when it comes to sponsored players, I am the only one that would even think of taking it easy on you. I hope you are getting better…this is my stop."

The next few stops are a blur. Once again Camila leaves me with plenty to think about. I approach my stop and prepare to exit. She left me with more questions than answers, but there was one thing she stated that is true. I need to continue to get better, and I will. It starts with Haven.

Chapter 9

LITMUS TEST

"Thought you got lost for a minute. I know you don't get out much."

Why is it that people always try to be funny at someone else's expense? That sounds a little strange coming from me. There are just times when it is just tired and old…and not funny. Normally, I'm not affected by Sedrick's off-target comedic attempts. Maybe I have just been around him too much over the past few weeks.

"Even if I don't, I still know my way around this city. Eh, if I'm not the last one here, how will everyone get to take in my greatness when I walk in the room?"

I can see Haven scoff at my comments. I don't care. Let the mind games begin.

"So you and Haven will be going best out of nine. No money involved just some friendly bragging rights."

"C'mon, Sed, you really think beating Darren is anything worth bragging about?" Haven seems to have jokes. Didn't see that coming.

"It will probably be the second best thing that's happened to you besides me being born to give you the opportunity to go against me." I couldn't just let him slide one in and think that's the end of it. I can do this all day!

"You're getting bold, Darren. I see those scrubs you have been set up to play is paying off." I'll let that comment slide. Now, all I want to do is to see his face after I beat him. I have the perfect line already lined up after I win.

Haven has always looked sharp. Even in this setting he sports his button-down with a sleek jacket, nice pants, and whoa...those shoes! This is the part of the game I don't understand. I know Haven is well-off, making plenty of money. Camila, on the other hand, was more down to earth, but maybe that's just her style. No flash, just get it done. I admire that. Even with his quip and debonair look, I couldn't wait until the end of the contest to serve him my fire.

"I'm learning quickly not to turn down easy money, Haven. Since you don't have to worry about that today, I'll only be taking your confidence."

"Okay, fellas, although I would like to see this go on for a bit. We are all friends here, so cut the talking and let's see what you got," Sedrick jumps in to squelch the flames. We are friends, but this is competition and we are not friends until it is over.

Haven doesn't know what he is getting himself into. I am a much better player than even I expected to be at this point. Haven wins the lag, but not by much. He chooses to go ball in hand. He doesn't realize I have a strategy for that.

"I love it! I'm going against a follower. That's fine, I'll dictate, you follow. You sure want that. I'll give you an opportunity to change your mind..."

"Like Sed said, talking is over, D. It's time to come out from behind the curtain."

My break is not as great as I expected it to be. I rebound and put my first three balls in with no issues. Haven knocks in his. I am looking to make quick work of the first game. I haven't seen Haven play, so I don't know his tactic. Neither of us wants to divulge too much strategy right now. I don't see him teaching me anything I don't already know. The game is not overly complicated; you just have to keep your emotions in check.

I sink a fourth ball and look at Haven. He doesn't look worried, but I know he is starting to feel the pressure. I pocket my fifth ball, and I am feeling good. I didn't do this well against lesser competition.

"You might want to reconsider having me break next game, pahtna!"

Haven quickly matches my shot and evens the game. "You haven't done anything I didn't expect after the break…just keep playing. You didn't set up your next shot very well, and now you are left with no options. I'm interested to see if you can get out of this. If you don't, you might as well put the stick down."

I think about Camila's shot when we played, and I attempt to jump his ball to knock in my own and fail miserably. I sloppily knock in my ball, but I hit his ball prior. This offers him a chance to put my ball back on the table where he chooses. It's an appropriate punishment for sloppy play. Haven begins with a long shot, unnecessarily I might add. He wears a confident smile that echoes the ensemble he has on.

I miss my next shot awkwardly. Haven is now down to one ball left compared to my two. I have a good shot to rebound since his last ball is in positioned along the head of the table against the rails. My cue ball sits sandwiched between his last ball and one of my last two balls with his cue ball serving as the bottom of the "T" formation that they currently form.

"Darren, I could go for my ball and attempt a difficult shot, but instead, I want the satisfaction of pocketing your ball."

He is setting up quickly and buries my cue ball in the corner pocket on the opposite end! A tremendous shot.

"I don't know about you Darren, but I'm as confident as ever!" His smile has never been more condescending.

I took my lumps from Haven losing 5–1 in the best out of nine. Sedrick was not lying. Haven is very good! If he is not even the best player, how the heck am I going to win this tournament?

"You did well, D. I have more experience than you, and let's be real with each other, I'm better than you. I will say, you played well and you are going to beat some people in this tournament if you keep improving. It just won't be me."

What is up with the wink thing? Why does he have to wink after he says it? I'm not as bad as I showed tonight. I'm not settling for second place to nobody.

"I want a rematch."

"You serious…right now?"

"Yeah, right now!"

"Don't think so. I have things to do, but it was good to see you again, D. If I don't see you until the tournament, I wish you luck. Keep practicing man, you're doing well."

"Wait, how 'bout this. If I don't see you in the final of the next tournament because you folded, I get my rematch and you hook me up with your sponsor...deal?"

Haven's laughter suggests this is not going to go my way. "I'm not into the game of being second place. *If* you win the tournament, I'll introduce you. If you don't win the final, no rematch."

"Deal!"

"Oh, and by the way, I'm not playing in the next tournament. I don't need the practice or the money." Only he would brush himself off after that comment. "You'll see me at the tables again when the big money is on the line. I earned my spot."

If he does that I'm-better-than-you wink one more time...I tell ya.

I walk over to Sedrick whose phone was more important than the match that was taking place. All I can think about is how I have to make the long trip back to the house after taking an 'L'. I liked when my uncle would say, "You can't take the 'L' and still have the lesson." He always thought the best lessons were learned through winning. I couldn't tell you what I took away from that beatdown.

"Can you actually give me a ride back or do I have to find my way because I lost?"

"I like that idea. Get to steppin'!" He laughs, but I don't.

"No, I'll take you. Sorry about being on the phone. I was trying to get you in a tournament in Europe, but that's not going to work out."

"I thought you already had me in one before the big one."

"I do, but it's about marketing man. The more people that see your skills, the more money it will bring in. We are going to have to update your wardrobe before the big one. You can't go in there looking like that."

"I don't care about looks, Sed; I'm just trying to win this thing."

"By the look on Haven's face, you didn't have much success against him tonight."

"Haven is legit! Mind games do not work on him. It's like he took what I said and just turned it on me."

"Yeah, that's what he does. Trash talk doesn't work with him. Try being quiet next time. Don't pay him any mind. That is when you may notice a difference. Haven't you noticed how into himself he is?"

"Just a little bit. Yeah, maybe I should have caught that…eh, Sed, I ran into a fellow Spikes player on the subway today."

"Anybody I would care about?"

"Probably not, but definitely someone you know. Camila."

Sed perks up. "Word! I see quite a few of these cats over time, especially when I'm hanging out over here. I haven't seen her yet."

"She wasn't over here; she got off a few stops before I got here."

"Knowing Camila, she didn't say much." I wonder how much anyone has tried to talk to her. The consensus is she is not a talker. The reasoning behind it is unknown. I question how many of these Camila experts have actually tried to communicate with her.

"That's the thing—she said enough. What's her story? What do you know about her?"

"Not much, she sticks to herself. She doesn't flaunt her winnings. When she does win, she just confers with her sponsor and goes."

"Is she single?" His look proves that Sedrick took this much differently than what my intention was.

"Are you trying to get with her dude?"

"No, no. I'm trying to find out if she is by herself. She doesn't seem to be like the other Spikes players I have played."

"Just don't go down that road. You are not the first to try. I'll tell you this. She is a big family person! She spends all her time with them. That's her life. That's pretty much all I know. She will probably be at the tournament before the big one. I haven't seen her miss one. One of the few that don't miss any. The woman is dedicated!"

I hope I don't explore something that is a dead end. I need to promise myself that if Camila does not want to let me in, then I need to respect that and move on. The approach is going to be important. She may be willing to have lunch with me. Make it nonthreatening. I need to stop letting the assortment of thoughts in my brain paralyze my intentions. They are unadulterated. I just need to have Camila understand this.

Chapter 10

OFFICE VISIT

Going to work is getting harder and harder to do since I have created a nice little stack of money on the side. Sed keeps me honest. He told me not to deposit any money just yet. Once I participate in the tournament or sponsored, any earnings would be provided through other means…or so I'm told. Sedrick plans to have some papers for me to sign prior to the tournament. I'm sure everyone reaches a crossroads with a job. I feel right now I have a lesser position in a company with the hopes of ranking up, but on the other hand, I could do something more lucrative with no benefits or long-term guarantees. It is a classic safe versus risk situation. At this point in my life and career, it is time to take a risk.

Hyung is my peer, coworker, and most importantly, I consider him a friend. He will be the one that gets stuck with the extra shifts until someone gets hired. I feel an obligation to tell him what is going on. It has only taken me half the shift before I could start discussing it with him.

"So I have been thinking, Hyung."

"Okay, that seems normal. Wasup?"

"I want to get your thoughts on this. I think I'm ready to move on from this job. I don't see a clear trajectory here. There are so many people over us, it would take forever before we raised in the ranks high enough that doing this is actually worth it long term."

"You think so, huh. Keep it in perspective. What other job lets you work out your hours, for the most part, provides you benefits, and allows you to pay enough bills to survive in a two-bedroom apartment before the age of twenty-three?"

"Well, we are older than twenty-three, that's the first thing, and second, the military comes to mind."

"Okay, I'll give you the military, but you do realize unless you are married, you will have to stay in the dorms, and they keep you there as long as they can. They want to keep an eye on you. They have cameras everywhere and everything. There is no privacy in that."

Hyung can go off the rails at times and this happens to be one of them. "This is crazy talk man, either way, neither one of us was thinking about going into the military. Much respect to all who join, but I'm going to go another route."

"Well, D, even if you refuse the comforts of here and the military, I wish you the best in the workforce wasteland that awaits you. I'll make sure the guy that replaces you is good, but just not quite that good until you tell me everything is okay with you, and then I'll make him great. Like I did with you!"

"Appreciate that." Hyung doesn't understand that I don't plan on ever coming back. That's the point of growth. You don't go back down.

"So what are you thinking of doing?"

"Well, with my current living situation, with my mom…"

"You mean being under her roof, right?"

"Yes, fool. Now let me finish…and my uncle passing, I have been doing a lot of thinking. If I'm going to take any risk in my life I should do them now, while I can physically, mentally, and organically recover."

"I'm not following the organic reference, but I appreciate your attempt at *omne trium perfectum*. There is symmetry to your response. It is known as the Rule of Three."

"Hyung, are you listening or looking for every opportunity to teach me something you learned from your night classes? The bottom line is I'm done. I'm putting in my two weeks' and taking a chance. Wherever my drive and effort takes me, then it takes me."

"It sounds a little irresponsible. Almost like Maslow's Hierarchy isn't important to you, but I respect you, Darren, and if anybody is going to break through and solve a nonexistent problem, it is you."

My smile is only because when Hyung is this extra, he is usually in an emotional place.

"I'll miss you too, my man. This might be our last shift, but I know how to reach you, and you know how to reach me. So we're good!"

"It won't be the same. Good luck to you! Now, let's get to the real reason you are leaving. You found out Stacy was going to say something about us, didn't you?"

The laugh I was sharing with Hyung was enjoyable while knowing a chapter was ending. He was right. As much as I say we will keep in touch. Things will not be the same. We never talked much outside of work. Hyung was a realist, even in his eighteenth century-esque contemporary montage way of stating it. If I'm going to start this leap, I need to at least create a backup plan, and I know just who to start with.

* * *

Myron talked a lot about how he could help me on my path. I was fortunate enough that he had a cancellation. Although I don't think I have any issues, I need to speak to him alone and with anonymity...well, at least until he sees me.

"Hello, I have an appointment to see Dr. Campbell."

"Is this your first time here?"

A confident nod suffices for this question.

"Okay, please sign-in at the kiosk, and I will call you up in a second to get you taken care of."

Why did I do this? Now I have to figure out how to even get past the receptionist without getting noticed. I should rescind my two-week notice right now. I'm already a fish out of water.

"Mr. Duncan?" My luck just turned in my favor. I hear the fake me called, and it is by the doctor himself.

"Yes, that's me."

It was like he had come face-to-face with his executioner. It is up to me to not allow his shock to turn into disdain. I can't address it out here, and I need to say something before he does.

"I'm so happy you had an opening; I have really been struggling the last few days. I need your help."

"Uh, sure, good to see you as well. Just follow me…Marcus."

At least he was willing to play along. He could have buried me where I stood. There is hope for me yet.

"What in the hell are you doing here? I have patients that actually *need* care. I hope this is important. Does your mom know you are here?"

Maybe this won't go as well as I thought it would.

"No, she doesn't. I do have a reason to be here. When we were at dinner you stressed the importance of figuring out what I wanted to do with my life. That is why I'm here. My mom doesn't know, but I quit the warehouse job. I wanted to see if you might have something I could get into. Entry-level of course. Anything that could get me in the door."

"I didn't know you had a fondness for my field."

"You got me thinking, but I'm not sure this is for me."

"I don't have any openings at this office right now. There is hope. While this is what I love, I do have other ventures in arenas such as real estate and supply procurement. I tell you what, Darren, I will make a few phone calls, and I will get back to you."

"I really appreciate it, Myron."

"Don't praise me yet, and if this does happen, your mom does not need to know I was involved."

"My mom wouldn't care if you were involved. It would probably score you a few points that I caused you to lose."

Myron is stepping closer to me, and it doesn't feel like a hospitable feeling. I feel the thickness of his fingers on my shoulder and his eyes scan my face and upper body to verify focus. His repellent stare is beginning to make me uncomfortable.

"There it is. That's what I was looking for. That moment when you realize you don't run a damn thing. What your mom and I have has nothing to do with you. It doesn't matter what you say. It doesn't

63

matter what you do. That's *my* woman. Now, as any good dad would do, I will help you, but if you try to come between us, you will wish you didn't. I will call you when I have more news. And the next time you decide to show up in my office…don't. You'll hear from me soon. Take care, son."

I hurriedly shrug his hand off on my shoulder and disengage from the temporary trance. Negative narrative intrudes my thoughts as I walk out of his office. The anger rises so much it floods any cognitive thoughts. Myron just showed me a side I knew in my core he had from the beginning. I didn't trust my instincts. He can save his phone call because I won't be asking him for help. I'm going to hustle my way up in Spikes. I'll take any and all matches I can until I somehow get sponsored.

My mom needs to know that Myron is not what he seems. There is no way to prove this. If I tell her that he offered me work, he would probably deny it, and then I would have to tell her about quitting my job. I can't do that just yet. I need to win this first tournament, get some more money in my pocket and show my mom that I have been saving. That wouldn't be a lie. I'm not comfortable flying into shady airspace by lying to my mom. It's all about pacing and timing. Just pace myself. The truth about Myron will reveal itself soon enough. It always does with people like him. I'll be patient and focus on me for a bit.

Chapter 11

MAKING RANK

After drudging through a slew of preparation matches, the tournament is finally here. My look says I spent too much money, but it's about time I look the part. I'm shooting for sponsorship, and they need to know I'm serious. When I step out of this room, it will be time to lock in. Just keep my emotions in check and I will be fine. As much as I wish Haven was here so I could give him the business, I understand Haven is not the ultimate goal.

Sedrick enters the bathroom like he chased bad sushi with spoiled milk. "Are you done staring in the mirror? Dang D, I know you want sponsors, but they're not looking for groupies, man. You ball out, and they will notice. You don't have to worry about that anymore, anyway."

"What do you mean?"

"Let's go. I need to show you the board and something else that'll have you go crazy." This is just what I need, a surprise right before my first tournament match.

"Okay, so let's look at the board. Remember what I said. In tournament matches, it is the best two out of three. You are lucky some of the great players bowed out in preparation for the Spikes equivalent to golf's Masters. There are still a lot of eyes here. Some players are here to watch, just to see the competition. You already know Haven, although he usually doesn't worry about any competition.

"There are sixteen competitors. There will be a brief break when we get to the final four players. Expect the noise to pick up as we get closer to the final game."

With the feeling in the room alone I can tell the stakes have been raised. The board has everyone listed by their tag.

"Sed, I don't see my name."

"Oh wait…yeah, it's there. Riiight there! Check this out!"

I traced the invisible bridge made by Sedrick's finger to a name on the board, but it wasn't mine. While still confused by my namesake not being represented, I turn to see Sedrick holding primo-looking Spikes equipment. The cue stick was pristine, highlighted with a black glossy matte finish. It has keys on a chain all over it with one golden key on the whole stick. Other keys are outlined with green and red. The cue ball has a black closed lock on it.

"That's all good Sed, but who does that belong to?"

"It's yours, bro! That's the surprise. You've been sponsored!" The rush of enthusiasm is tempered by skepticism.

"I thought I had to compete in a tournament first?"

"You have had a buzz since you beat Spades. I guess someone finally pulled the trigger. This right here is the small stuff. This is the surface. The clothes, the stick, and cue ball. This could be life-altering man. It also means you don't have to worry about your money no more. You are considered clean. You don't know it, but you are on a company's payroll even though you don't work there. Dope, right?"

Breathing seems to be a little harder at this moment. I'm sponsored! That's exciting and overwhelming. With sponsorship come expectations. The scary thing is I don't know what the expectations are. I always plan to win, but when my play affects another person's bottom line, how will I perform? I'm at the show now. I can't have these thoughts.

"Sed, tell me who it was so I can thank them and then move on. I have to get ready for my first match."

"It was a lady…late forties, maybe early fifties. I haven't seen her before. She sought me out and knew my tag. Said to make sure you get these and ensure I passed on her congratulations to you. I asked what her name was and she said, Emily or Evee or something. It was hard to make out. She told me that if you won, you would meet soon. It was crazy cryptic and standard for this business. Don't sweat it though, just take care of business, and I'll use my connects to see what I can find out."

"Thanks, Sed. I really appreciate you looking out."

"Any time and every time, D, you know that."

Sed put me at a measure of ease. I took a deep breath and examined the board once again. It's going to take some time to get used to "Lock." Your tag is chosen for you in this game. The best part is I get to baptize this baby right now. I see I'm a 13 seed which is motivation in itself, but I also see Spades is a 3 seed! Why would she be ranked higher than me? I beat her one on one.

"Sedrick, how do these rankings work? I beat Spades, how is she higher than me?"

"Because she has put in more work than you. I can't describe the algorithm that goes into it. It's like trying to figure out how they decide one team is ranked higher than another in college football. It's a level of arbitrariness to it for sure. The rankings don't matter though. You are in it, now you have to…"

"Don't say it, Sed. Please spare me and don't say it."

"Don't say what?"

"Let's just leave it right there. I'm not in the mood for a cliché rhyme."

"Whatever. You are going against Anvil in the first match. Here, take your weapon and go put in work. I'll be watching from afar, but I need to scout the competition."

Sed can see that I'm distracted. I take a step forward and feel Sed's hand on my shoulder.

"One shot at a time, D. It's in you, I know it."

I nod to him and he begins to walk away. I look over at the table, and it is quite obvious who Anvil is. He's a stocky individual who looks at me like I'm threatening his life. He's not happy about it either. I never let bully tactics distract me, so why start now.

The game starts well for me. Anvil has hit some quality shots and things are even. Anvil prefers risk and I need to find a way to use this predictable macho tactic to my advantage. I've never went against anyone in pocket billiards that anchors balls like he does. He freezes it right against the cushion. That's not a viable strategy against me. His obsession with it causes my aiming line to go unaffected. I am able to hit my shots clean and without many problems. I'm all settled in now—starting to feel natural. I realize this player can't beat me. I wonder was this what Haven thought about me. Let me make sure I finish this guy off and then I can think about it.

"D, great match! You made that look eeaasy! I know Anvil is more of a banger, but he still got sponsored. I once saw him break and run Bentley right off the table. Haven't seen him do it since though."

Did Sed just give me a compliment or a lesson on how not to give a compliment? I don't care. I won, and it feels good.

"I figured if they are in this tournament, they are sponsored. His play style made it a pretty chill match for me. I picked up on his strategy early."

"That's what I'm talking about. You're the Einstein of this game, man. Look, I just wanted to let you know that the competition is okay here, but nothing too formidable. I wouldn't be surprised if you end up in the final with Spades."

"Spades? How is she doing?"

"Spades is driven, dude. She hasn't dropped a game yet. 4–0 in her two matches! She is heading into the semis."

"There is something about her, Sed. I can't shake. She has some mystery to her."

"You're attracted to mystery, D! What happens once you find out, detective? Would she no longer be attractive? I hope you don't let that misguided love criteria take you to a place you don't want to go."

"I just want to know more. She's attractive and private. I like that. It's not about her mystery. It's like she is always thinking and plotting. Someone like that knows what they want." This is counter to how I am.

"Well, you better focus on wanting to beat Upstream. She is the best player in this tournament regardless of rankings. Everyone knows they need to play their best when she is behind."

"Oh, I get it. So she is a slow starter and strong finisher."

"Very strong!"

As the field shrinks, other players are now watching. I had Upstream down 1–0. She is possessed in game two. She is constantly making my shots difficult even when she didn't make her own. Now, we are tied up at 1–1. The third game is not as contentious. I am able to capitalize on ball misplacement and easily make some intermediately difficult shots. While Upstream still has four balls on the table, I finish it. Another match victory, and as I receive more pats on the back, I begin to see more chatter amongst the sponsors. The name and look of my own sponsor remains foreign. I look over and make eye contact with Camila. There couldn't be a worse time to try and engage in a conversation with her. That is exactly what I plan to do.

"Hi, uh, Spades."

"Hiya, Lock," Camila seems different right now. I will take her humor attempt as a positive invite. She continues, "Do you like your name?"

"Not at all, but I didn't choose it."

"Well, you should embrace it. It fits you." Her eyes sparkle with every word. It's hard for me to disengage.

"How so?" I don't know if I could mummify a question any more than that one. Maybe she won't notice.

"Even I have noticed first-hand the look you get when you focus in this game. I haven't seen someone that, dare I say it, *locked in*. Just look how determined you are to find out about me." Seriously! I am not that obvious.

"What makes you say that? I'm just trying to get to know a fellow competitor. I had a good match with you."

"You had a game with me, not a match. It was only good for you. But that's about to change today."

"I don't see how it will be different. I'm so much better than I was then." The nature of this conversation changed quickly.

"Yeah, I know. And this time I'm not going to let you win."

"Wait, let me win! You didn't let me win..."

Camila walked away as intermission is over. I know she didn't let me win. That's an easy thing for an opponent to say once they take a loss. She's just bitter. I'll make sure to put the rubber stamp on my win next time.

"Spades, Spades!"

I can't believe she turned around. It probably would have been better if she didn't.

"Do me a favor, don't lose."

No words. Just turned away from me like I'm the fifth member of a boy band. I'm not going to let her set me off. I'm going against a player that wasn't expected to be here. A 16 seed that beat the 1 seed. He's playing well today. I wonder what Sed has to say about this guy.

"What are you doing over here? You need to go to your table and get ready!" Sed blurts out like I'm trying to avoid the table.

"I'm headed that way, Sed. I just had a question about my opponent. It's the 16 seed."

"Got you, got you. So yeah, *Silence* is trash. He is not on your level, and if you lose a game to this clown, you may not get an invitation to the main tournament."

"What? This dude beat the 1 and 8 seed!"

"Yep, and you know what they won't be getting…an invite to the tournament. I'm telling you, this guy is not worthy. He's a very low-tier sponsor player that wouldn't make it out of the first round of the next tournament. I'm just telling you, D. You lose to this guy, you might as well go ask for more hours at the warehouse."

"Not happening. Thanks."

Sed looked very suspicious in the corner, but I'm sure he has to talk to some questionable characters in order to find out information about my sponsor. Either way, if my goals are to stay intact I need to go smash this dude!

2–0! That was easy work. I could feel myself slip into the zone easily and naturally those two matches. If I find that consistently, it doesn't matter who I go against. The best part about this is Camila won 2–0 as well. This couldn't have worked out better.

"D, now you get—"

"Camila, I know. I don't need any advice for this one. I remember the intel from the first match. First rule, force her to break. I'm cool this time around."

"Okay, Mr. Know-it-all. I'll be gone then."

Sed steps away, and I see Camila putting her glove on. Maybe this is when Spades takes over. I still can't make out what the saying is on her glove.

"Spades, before we start, I have a question…what is that saying on your glove?

"*Amo a mi familia*. It means, *I love my family*."

"Pretty cool. You will need more than love for this match." My attempt at amusement hit dead space. Camila quickly gave me a stare coupled with the roll of the eyes that instantly ported me to the outside of an inner circle. I didn't mean it to be a personal attack, but it's too late to go back.

I win the lag and force her to break. She was visibly upset. Camila is hungry. She definitely seems to have a different attitude this time around. No matter how ravenous she looks and plays this time around, I still don't believe she let me win our previous bout. Making this win more convincing is a must!

A sweep was quickly out the door as Camila wins the first game. A tightly contested second game ends with me being the winner. Now I have a situation reset. Although this won't be a dominate win for me, this is how it was meant to be. I just need to win. Something I have done against her already.

Camila wins the lag for the first time. She looks at me and smirks. I must not be worthy of the decency of a smile. She then decides to break which completely throws me off. I look over at Sed, and he is as perplexed as I am. Her break is not very good and she knows it.

The break has not broken her focus. We are going shot for shot. She is not even trying to block my shots. It is almost like she is trying to prove a point. That would explain the break. Spades is relentless! She has made one great shot after another. We are both down to two balls left with her in a position to truly finish me off. It would be difficult for me to make my shot given the position of her cue ball being frozen against the rail next to one of my object balls. I decide to cheat the pocket. This in-turn makes her shot a lot trickier with my ball sitting right there on the side of the pocket.

Camila decides to take aim at my cue ball. She is going to go for the victory here. The shot she is attempting is one I wouldn't even attempt. The worst part is she will lose a turn if she misses.

She made it…I lost! My body hollows out. The feeling of nothing postpones any congratulatory praise. Could it be possible Spades was right? Maybe she did let me win. First Haven, and now to lose in the final. Not only do I not get my rematch with Haven, but I lose money and lose to someone I have beaten *and* I lose a better payout.

"D, don't worry about it. This was more of a Calcutta than a sponsor-based event. It's hard to say that about any Spikes tournament. Two good things come out of this: You don't need to be introduced to Haven's sponsor now, and most importantly, it's the next one you want to at least be in the finals in. Being in the finals makes you more money than if you won this tournament three times over."

I could feel the temperature rising from within. Taking any condolence for a lost is not happening. "I'm going to win it, Sed. Don't worry about that."

I look over at Camila, and my temperature begins to regulate. I walk over to Camila to congratulate her. She beat me fair. She actually looks either interested to talk to me or satisfied.

"Hey, Spades."

"I'm only tolerating you calling me that because of where we are. Once these tournaments are over, just talk. Don't call me by my tag. Okay."

"Okay, gotcha. I can work on that." There really is no working on anything, just doing. "I have a serious question. Did you really let me win the first time?"

"Yes, I did."

There goes my temperature again. I can't believe she is still sticking with that story. What about our conversation on the train? She said I had a look—a focus. I knew what she was talking about, but I can't let this go.

"Really? Well…consider us even now." A quick quip may save pride only.

"Oh, okay," her laugh confirms her thoughts. She knows what I already know. "Well, thanks for *letting* me win."

She is taking this too well. I'm not going to concede anything.

"You might not believe it, but I did. After that first game…I thought I needed to make it more competitive. It will make the major tournament that much more special."

"Lock, you're not perfect. That's okay. I'm just as driven as anyone else, but outside these walls I have other concerns. Other needs that must be taken care of."

"You are good at turning this thing on and off. I don't get how to read you."

"Don't try to read me. That's part of your problem."

"Well, do you think we can get together sometime and discuss the other parts of my problem?"

"Yeah, I think so." She recognizes my corny line. I appreciate her conscious decision not to bury me where I stand.

"If you're free Wednesday night, how 'bout we meet at Franco's?" Using the seemingly last bit of confidence I had, I now cringe waiting for her response.

"Not a fan, but I'll meet you there."

"Cool. Maybe I should let you win more often."

"Bye, Lock."

"See you Wednesday."

Camila actually let a smile go and in my direction. A loss never felt so good.

Chapter 12

FOUR-COURSE MEAL

My mom wants another "family familiarity" dinner. She told me the words I knew would be coming one day. She thinks she is falling in love with Myron. I couldn't dare tell her what had happened. Not yet. I feel like the roles have reversed. Now I'm the protective parental figure. My original thoughts on Myron have been certified true—a new way to rid myself of him has to take place. The best starting point is to get him talking, maybe he will give something up.

"Darren, come on down. Myron just called, he is five minutes away." My heart stopped for a second, hoping he would cancel. I trudge down the stairs toward the kitchen table carrying two hundred pound barbells for legs.

"Need my help with anything, Ma?"

"No, you just go ahead and have a seat. The wine is poured and I'm about to take the asparagus out of the wok."

The doorbell rings, and I feel organs sink to the bottom of my stomach.

"I got it, Ma." I still need to exude confidence. He can't have an edge. Not tonight.

"Hey, Darren. Good to see you again." He hands me his coat. I want to drop it immediately. Instead, I decide to drag half of it on the ground before I place it in the coat closet. It was the next best thing.

"Darren, pick up his coat!"

"Oh, sorry, Ma. I didn't realize." I absolutely realized it!

My mom gave him a massive hug. I had to look away and pretend as if I was about to take my seat.

"Hey, baby. You doing okay?"

"Much better now that I'm going to get your cooking." Every word he says feels like a needle prick.

Dinner is going as expected. It can't stay quiet for long. It would be better if I break the silence. That way I can dictate the conversation.

"So, Darren." Too late. "How are things at the warehouse? Anything new since our last talk?" I never wanted to snatch a fork out of someone's mouth and stab them with it more. He has put me in a tight position. I am forced to tell my mom the truth or lie. My hesitation to start the conversation is now costing me.

"It's not going that well, but I have saved enough money from that job. I plan to move on soon. That's what I wanted to talk to you about, Ma. I should be moving out in the next month. I have enough for a deposit and a couple of months of rent."

"So you quit your job at the warehouse?" Myron is really testing my gangsta right now. I need to put him on notice.

"You do realize I was talking to my mom, right? I would appreciate it if you didn't interrupt. I don't know about you and *your* values, but the way I was raised, that's kinda rude."

"My apologies, Darren." He wipes off his lips and readies his next knifing words. "That was rude of me. I understand how you feel. It is like lying to your parents. I could never do it. No matter what I did. Whenever they asked me about something I knew I did wrong, I always felt compelled to tell them. Brittany, I just want to say you have raised quite the son. Good manners, doesn't lie. You don't see that often. Let's toast to that."

Dinner ends as contentious as it started. My mom did not seem affected by what had transpired one bit this time around. And then I locked eyes with her.

"Darren, help me with the dishes in the kitchen."

"Brit, I'll be happy to help clean up?"

"No, you are fine, Myron. Me and this boy got it. Thank you though."

Knowing him, if he really wanted to help, he wouldn't ask. There is no doubt he got the better of me at dinner, but it's not over. This charade is going to come to an end tonight. I'll make sure of this as soon as I help my mom in the kitchen.

"You know how I feel about Myron, right?" My mom was not making eye contact with me. She just continued to wash the dishes.

"Of course, Ma."

"Then why does it seem like you are trying to make Myron feel as uncomfortable as can be? You never talked to someone more senior than you like that. Knowing how I feel, I really didn't expect that from you."

"You're right, Ma, and I'm sorry. I just feel like there is a lot we don't know about him."

"Well, what would you like to know?" This could be a surprise opening that I was looking for. I could be made privy to more intel and potential ammunition that could be put to use.

"Tell me about him. Has he been married? Does he have kids? Where is he from? There is a lot to know."

"I appreciate you caring, but you don't have to be my dating screener. You don't think your mama would ask these same questions? You think that less of me?"

"No, Ma."

She is right. I have made this a little personal, but I still need to get this information.

"Sooo, will you tell me?" A smile at the end will hopefully lighten the mood.

"Sure, he does not have kids and his mother still lives in North Carolina. That's where he is from. He has lived up here for the majority of his life. He has worked hard for everything he has just like me."

"Was he married previously?"

"Good lord, Darren… Yes, he was. You happy?"

"I'm sorry, Ma. Thank you."

"Can you stop cutting up now?"

"Yes, Ma." I love the smile my mom gives after a convincingly negative comment. It makes me smile. "If you don't mind, I'm going to go apologize to Darren."

"I wouldn't expect anything less, go ahead."

I had no intentions on apologizing, but this conversation is past overdue.

"Hey, Myron. You have a moment? My mom said she was going to be a minute. We can go in the living room."

"Not a problem." His body language confesses to him knowing what this was going to be about.

The living room will provide us some security from my mom overhearing anything. It is probably best since even in my own house, better known as my mom's house, I feel like I'm on the defense.

"So you were married? Tell me—"

"Before you continue, I have a question for you. How did you like it?"

"Like what?"

"The new stick and cue ball. You like it?"

How does he know about that? My mom could have told him I liked to play pool. She could have bought me something that I don't know about yet. I'm not showing my cards on this one.

"I don't know what you mean."

"That game doesn't work with me. You'll find that out sooner or later. I hear you performed well at the tournament."

He does know. I don't know how or why, but he knows.

"I did. My turn. How do you know about the tournament? How did you know I was in it?"

"Let me answer one question at a time. I get around Darren. Even in a big city such as this, I know a lot about the dark underbelly that exists. This tournament is a light amongst the darkness. The rich can get richer and those that are struggling can rise to prominence. It's a win-win! The proprietor of Spikes brought me a long a while ago. This was when we operated out of one location. The game is growing exponentially; I'm not sure we will be able to keep it the way it is. Too many people, too much money won and lost. Eventually, that will draw attention. My advice to you is to play the short game. Get in and get out. This is not a long-term answer. Does that answer your question?"

"Not the second one."

"I knew you were in it because I sponsor you. I wouldn't be a responsible sponsor if I didn't know your whereabouts. I always have someone keeping an eye out on my investments. All of them."

Whenever a thought crosses my mind that the situation could not get worse, it gets worse. I'm too shocked to be angry. A flummoxed expression flashes like a neon sign and I can't pull the plug. He won't stop talking and I can't break free from my vocal shackles.

"I'm really glad we could have this talk because there are a few expectations I want to discuss with you."

"I don't give a damn about your expectations." Finally, I manage to speak. "I don't want this. I'm done with Spikes. I'm not competing in the tournament. I don't know who you paid or how much you paid, but you wasted time and money sponsoring me."

"I'm going to have to disagree with pretty much all that you said. It's not going to happen. Have you heard of Fireball?"

"Are you serious? No, I don't know all these tags for these players."

"Well, you knew Fireball quite well. An outgoing man and tremendous Spikes player. A little overconfident at times…and was not good with money, although he made plenty of it. He incurred some debt due to his overconfidence and couldn't pay it back. It became a sad slippery slope, because no player leaves this game with an unhappy sponsor or proprietor."

"This has nothing to do with me. Save these clown stories for some other fool."

"Hey, is everything okay?" My mom's antenna must have been going off.

"Oh yeah, Brit, we are fine. Your son was just expressing his interest in working for me. I was letting him know that there was a spot available. Not at my clinic, but my supply depot where he could make triple the money and a potential benefits package based on performance."

"That sounds like a lot to think about. Thank you, Myron, but you didn't have to do that."

"No, you didn't, Myron." An apprehensive and unsupportive response was the best I could muster.

"It's not a problem at all. I do what I can to help people get a solid professional start. It's up to them to take advantage of it at that point." Our contentious eyes meet up.

"I'll leave you two to finish, but don't be back here all night."

"We just need a couple more minutes and we will be done, Brit. I can go over all the details another time. That's if he accepts the offer."

It was cringing to hear the words coming out of his mouth. Like he is some philanthropist. When truly he is only looking to line his own pockets. My mom walks away appearing to be happy about it.

"I'm not a storyteller. This isn't fiction. I don't have time for games if they don't make money. There is a debt to be paid here. A debt that is currently owed by you."

"Me? Impossible! All I have been doing in this game is win."

"Last I saw, you were losing to Spades, and shockingly, the ignorance is a little surprising and sad. I'm going to have to be blunt with you. You do owe Fireball's debt. Oh, and the expectation is that you must win the next tournament in order to pay it back in full. That's one of the reasons I took the flier on you. Fireball was a legend. The thought of having someone related to him fighting to pay off his debt was a fascinating find."

"Related?"

"Oh yeah, don't get me wrong. Your mom is growing on me and all, but she was just a way to you. I didn't expect for you to show up at my work so soon. That was just a bonus for me. Your uncle, what's his name, Reggie. You seem to know so little, but your friend, Sedrick, knows it all. Doesn't seem right."

My mind is swimming, I can't see straight, and I feel like I am being hit with haymaker after haymaker. Mom comes in the room at exactly the wrong time for me.

"Okay, break it up. Y'all can finish this conversation another time. You are now on my time. Myron and I have a movie to catch."

"I believe we are all set here. Darren was telling me that his friend Sedrick needs a stable job too. I told him to give him a call. That should make him more comfortable in his decision. I'll call and catch up with you soon, Darren."

Myron wants me to call Sedrick. What does Sedrick know about all this? I can't hold off this pain inside. To know my mom is with someone that doesn't return authentic love back is heartbreaking. On top of that, there is so much information that needs to be processed. Now that I don't have Myron in front of me, I have to call Sedrick. Hopefully he can make some sense out of this.

Now that mom and Myron have left the house, I'm calling Sed.

"Wasup, D?"

"That's what I need you to answer. You remember when the lady came up to you and you thought she said Emily or Evee? Well, it was actually initials. Those initials stand for MC, as in Myron Campbell."

"Word! That guy *is* one of the sponsors. I don't see him much though."

"He is also dating my mom."

"Oh, hell no! I mean, it's great that he sponsored you, but dating your mom too? This guy's on some other stuff man."

"Apparently, he has a reason too. He said that I owe a debt."

"That's impossible, bro. You just started playing. What debt is he talking about?" I was happy to hear Sedrick's response. Myron implicated that Sedrick knows about this. However, the fact that he mentioned Sedrick means he knows something.

"Sed, that's what I said! He said I owed a debt that my Uncle Reggie owed. He went by the tag, Fireball. This is extortion!"

"D, you believe that? This is an underground game that has shady seeds implanted all over. These guys have to have something over people. Think about it. How else can they keep them quiet? There are very few players that appear to not be indebted to their sponsors for one reason or the next."

"What about you, Sed? What do they have over you?"

"I have debt just like anyone else. I need to get rid of this debt in order for Briana and I to have a future. Hell, in order to have a future at all, I need to get out of this debt," Sed expresses definitively.

"So Spikes is your sole income, huh?"

"It is…I'm constantly grinding. So I have my side hustles, but this is the main bread and butter. This is my talent. This is my skill. I plan to ride it as long as I can. It might be a questionable profession, but I am gaining some deep connections with some powerful folks. Even if this game crumbles, I'm setting myself up for employment afterwards."

"You don't think when this game crumbles, they won't look to tie up loose ends…you included?"

"That's why I'm connected, D! I'm making sure to get your name out there too! We will be good. I promise you. I wouldn't bring you into this if your life would eventually be on the line. Believe that!"

"What happens once we are out of debt? How are they going to keep us from talking?"

"They can't keep anyone from talking. But I can give you an example of debt-free. Haven! He is debt-free and is making major money. Why would he want to mess that up? I look at it like this. We are no different than any athlete out there. We found something we are good at and the competition drives us. It's real good money, why wouldn't you keep doing it?"

"All I know is that I need to get Myron out of my life. If I win this tournament, I need to dump him as my sponsor. How can I make that happen?"

"That's going to take a conversation with the creator. That's the only possible way. Understand, what you are trying to do is unprecedented. Be ready to be denied or even worse, the creator may not want to talk to you," Sedrick's sedated tone is not of someone that is in a hurry to help.

"Are you able to setup a meeting for me?"

"I'll try, D. It is rare to get in his audience, but I'll try."

"Thanks, Sed."

Chapter 13

MEET AND GREET

I hope Camila didn't leave. I picked the worst day to be running behind. I probably could have selected a better location than Franco's. The company you keep can make anywhere worth being even if it is only for a brief moment in time. If Camila feels the same way, this will go well.

As I approach I can see that Camila is already here. She is standing outside, gently and innocently scanning people walking by between the more focused attentions to her phone.

"Hi, Camila. Sorry I'm late."

"A few more minutes, and I was out of here. Then I thought… I'm not going to pass on a free meal."

"Free meal? I never said…anyways, I got you. Yep, your money is no good here. I will pay for everything, this time."

Franco's is pretty busy today. I spotted a small booth in the back that would be the perfect setting for us. It is out of the way and not too intrusive. I just hope the bathrooms are not too active today.

"I'm glad you didn't stand me up, Camila…" The words ran out of my mouth before I could grab them. The ensuing gulp going down my throat registers the nerves.

"You're really going to start with that?"

"Would you rather me start with how I still haven't gotten over the fact that you beat me?" Truth is a better recovery than keeping the conversation on the fringes.

"I actually like that one better." She takes a quick sip of her drink and locks back on to me. I guess I am still required to drive this conversation.

"What do you think about Spikes?"

"You don't listen, do you? You don't suppose to talk about the game when you are out like this, and look at you. Have you always disregarded rules?" Camila says.

"I don't see it that way. It is more how I interpret the rule. It's fine, I'll start then. The better I get at this game, the more I see how the players are nothing more than servants to these so-called sponsors."

"I wouldn't call it servants, Darren."

"What would you call it then? They hold money over your head until you are able to pay it back. It seems like by the time you pay it back, people enjoy the lifestyle so much, they stick with their sponsors and keep making them money. That's servitude in a twisted and addictive way. My sponsor is dating my mom, how twisted is that? Tell me that is normal." Camila doesn't even know me, but I just clued her in on my situation. She gives off this aura when I'm close to her. I feel a true comfort in her presence.

"Wow! That's not normal, but let me tell you something. First, it's not always money they hold over you. If you are already good at billiards, they will find you. After they find you, they need to find out about you. If they can find something to bury you in this game, they will."

"You make it sound like there is no way out."

"There is always a way out, Darren. Nobody is getting out unless the debt is paid. I don't plan on doing this forever. I can't put this on a resume, and there is no guarantee the fake job they have me in will even hold up once this crumbles." Camila's pointed words shows her awareness on a deeper level than I thought. It does not answer the question why she is still in this, but it does make me question quitting my job at the warehouse.

"You mentioned they don't always use money. What do they have over you, Camila?"

"I don't want to talk about it."

"Well, I'll tell you this. I just found out that I am responsible for a debt as well. A debt I didn't even know about until after the last tournament."

"You might not think they knew about the debt, but someone knew. It usually starts with whoever introduced you to the game. That person may be a sponsor or it could be a runner for someone more powerful. Very rarely do sponsors make the first contact. Sponsors become more handsy when their prized possessions start winning."

"That can't be true for all situations. Sed helped me out. I was in a bad place and he wanted me to get out of the house. That led me to this money game. I thanked Sedrick for that. I've known him forever; he wouldn't do what you suggest."

"I'm not suggesting your friend did anything. I'm just telling you what happens. Not all situations are equal. I'm sure Sedrick had the best intentions with you. You just need to keep your eyes open."

"Like you did." Maybe I shouldn't have said that. "I mean, I don't understand how you are into this game. You don't seem to enjoy it." Camila grips her silverware and her look is reminiscent of our initial encounter.

"That's because I don't. I'm not into sports. It's not about the competition. I'm a fighter. I fight for my family. That's what is important, and that's who needs me." She sits back in her seat and breaks eye contact. She doesn't know this but I can relate to her struggle.

"So it's about your family. Me too! Did they leave you with a steep price to pay?"

"No, Darren! My *abuela* is here illegally along with seven other members of my family. They are all on the cusp of being deported if I don't perform well enough for my sponsor. The money I make pays for our entire household. I am so close to meeting my sponsors set goal so they are free. Then I will be free of this game. I don't relish in beating anyone, because I know they have a price to pay too. When I met you, you were different. You were not wearing a burden so the second time we met I wanted to prove a point to you. Now I know, you kinda understand."

"Once you pay off your debt for your family is your family promised US citizenship or a working visa or some other freedom promise by your sponsors?"

"Yes. The stakes are so high in this next tournament that if I win it, I will be able to pay off the remainder of my debt and finally be done with this. Are you in the same situation?"

"Yes, I have a debt to pay as well. I'm not sure how much it is. I just know I need to win this tournament to help. At least I thought that before now." It just hit me out of nowhere. Possibly I could work something out with Camila so we can both be winners at the end of this. "How about I make a deal with you Camila? If I get to the final, I will let you win, because you need this more than me."

"Here you go with the let you win thing again, huh."

"This time I'm telling the truth. This is wrong and although I'm not in a position to fix this I want to help you out."

"So what happens when you talk to another player and they tell you that they need to play for their husband or wife that is dying of cancer…they are out there too. Or maybe someone who says their child's medical bills must be paid? You can't keep blowing matches to help someone else out. I learned this a while ago. In the end, there will be more suffering than satisfaction. Most of us have come to grips with it. Some of us are just greedy after achieving our goals and want more. You will not know everyone's story, and you shouldn't. It will cloud your judgement. Focus on your goals, your freedom. I gotta run. Thank you, but sorry I couldn't finish lunch, if only we could have started earlier." She quickly rises from the table and heads towards the door. How am I supposed to continue this conversation? I don't know where she lives, her phone number, nothing!

"Can you leave me your number so we can talk later?"

"I'll see you at the tournament." Camila playfully dismisses my overture.

"You hardly talk at the tournament."

Her last smile said it all. She doesn't want to get involved in a relationship right now. After what she said, I don't blame her. How could I be so naïve about what Spikes truly is? For every guy like Haven, there is someone like Camila.

I'm glad I decided to take this walk. It was something I really needed. I see Suds with a small contingent of her believed associates doing exactly what her namesake is…drinking. This just shows you can't trust what some people say. I want to say hi, but I don't know her real name. I'll just wave and nod and see what happens.

"Hey, Darren! Come on over," The look the other people at the table have is not very inviting.

"I'm actually looking to clear my head, so I'm gonna keep moving."

"That's exactly what I'm doing right now. C'mon, just for a sec."

Suds orders me a drink, and I feel the pressure pulling me toward the empty seat beside her.

"Glad you could join us." A quick sheepish look at the table proves they don't show the same enthusiasm as she does.

"Sorry, I didn't ask what you wanted to drink, Darren. I figured you were in favor of the simple domestic type," I find it interesting that she knows my name. "Was I right?"

"You weren't wrong. Since we are throwing out names…"

"Liz, Liz Kelly. Sorry, I keep my ear to the ground so I pay attention to others while they constantly overlook me. It has served me well. I have placed high enough in tournaments. Still haven't made a finals like you did."

"How'd you know?"

"C'mon, Darren. Word gets around."

I hear one of her friends ask about the tournament and wonder what her response will be. For this game to be so underground there sure is a lot of covert chatter about it. I can see why Myron believes the word will get out soon enough. Too many people with loose lips.

"We play in an online hold 'em tournament together. Pretty intense too. I didn't participate in the last one but saw the final table. This guy is pretty good." Good save by Liz.

"So, Liz, will you be in the next tournament?"

"Oh, this is the largest field I have seen. It is the equivalent of March Madness! I'm not missing this one. If I only win one tournament, this is the one I want to win."

"I'm sure you will put down a few before that tourney."

"You know me!" She raises her glass as if offering a toast before taking a few drinks.

"I was surprised to see you out drinking considering what you told me."

"Well, don't believe everything you hear. I'm not entitled to tell you the truth, right? It's up to you to decide what is fact and what is fiction. I like to have fun with it, keep everyone guessing. That's what's interesting."

While she is right about the "interesting" part of that statement, it makes me less inclined to be around her. Someone who embraces lying as part of their moral fabric is on the same level as Myron Campbell. That is not my type of person.

"Sounds like you play a lot of games, Liz. Thanks for the drink, I need to get going."

"Darren, here, take my number. There's something you need to know about this tournament. Call me, if you want to know."

"How do I know if you have anything to say when I can't tell when you are lying or telling the truth. This might not even be your number."

"Trust your instincts. If I don't hear from you, that's cool and I wish you good luck. If I do, you'll be thankful that you did."

I am feeling a sweat coming on just thinking about all this. The goal now is to avoid any other familiar faces while I try and decompress. Stepping away from Suds today was the best decision I made. Volatile personalities are difficult for me to be around right now. I'm hoping Sed comes through and gets me that meeting with the ringleader of this Spikes game. I need answers.

Chapter 14

MY UNCLE'S KEEPER

It took a while to get to sleep last night. I don't think a nuclear bomb would have waked me once I did. I feel better today. Sedrick contacting me this morning has a little to do with that. Once again, he comes through for me. Although there are many questions I would like to address with the creator of Spikes, I need to stay on topic. My heartbeat can't be louder than my words. The drama around this game keeps thickening the closer this tournament gets. What was once believed to be my debt alone is no longer true. There are others including Camila that face these situations. Also, what info could Liz have that she needs to tell me? I don't know what pointers about the game Suds could really provide especially since she hasn't even made it to a final in any tournament. And then there is Myron Campbell. The threats or potential threats are all around. A knock at the door interrupts my thoughts. It's Sedrick.

"Okay, D. You will have about five minutes, tops. The question you will ask is, how do I switch supervisors? You will have to read between the lines for obvious reasons. If you say anything that is off-topic, expect a dumbfounded response. Never mention the game, tournaments, tags, or anything like that. He's smart. He will pick up on replacement references. You got it? Oh, and no names!"

"Yeah, Sed, I got it," I wasn't sure how well I got it. Sed's high-strung run-through of what not to do brought the butterflies back.

"Although, it seems like this whole conversation is about replacement references. Let's just make the call."

"Cool, here we go."

Sed looks at me as he dials the number. I noticed the phone he was using was not his. He verbally swats away any attempts to ask about it as we wait for an answer. On the fourth attempt, someone picks up, but it is nothing but silence. Sedrick looks at me as if I was blowing my opportunity.

"Hi, sir, I have a quick question." The returned silence implored me to continue. "I was...I was wondering how I could switch supervisors?"

"While usually I reserve to answer these workplace dilemmas in-person, I understand you have unusual circumstances for this request. I do not take lightly the unethical behavior of our supervisors, and I will make sure all supervisors are reminded of the severe consequences of mistreating our employees."

"I never mentioned that the issue was unethical."

"Please accept my apology, an associate of yours had informed me of the details and assured me of the accuracy after investigation by our HR department. Was this request about a transfer due to improper actions by your supervisor?"

"Yes, but there is more to this. I have a new allotment that is going to take a long time to pay off. I would like a raise to help me cover this cost. It would help me greatly."

"I was made aware of this allotment when provided an overview of your situation. I will tell you that we do offer specific employee performance bonuses that may suit your needs. There will need to be an assessment of your contributions prior to any permanent action being taken. I will consider your request, and you will hear from a rep soon."

"Thank you, one last thing." Sedrick is threatening to rip the phone from my hand. "I heard you were fond of the company that this allotment belongs to. I used to have a close relationship with them, but not any longer."

"Yes, it was a great company that assisted many people, including your associate. Unfortunately, they are not as viable as they once were. There are a few reasons for that. Reasons your associate has first-hand knowledge of. It is a sad story, but it could be one of triumph in the end. I have to get going; it was a pleasure to be able to go over your issue, and it is always a priority to ensure our employees are taken care of. If you have any further questions, don't hesitate to ask. I'll see you in the office soon."

The references to my associate had to be for Sedrick. These were the same volleys that Myron threw to me. Sedrick claimed not to have any knowledge of my debt. Sedrick's sunken eyes and lowered head provide me with an uncomfortable reality.

"What was that all about, Sed? This is the second time you have been brought up when it comes to this debt. What was your involvement? Tell the truth…for once."

"Look, don't act like you're perfect! I racked up lots of debt, Darren. I had debt that I came to the game with and got even more while trying to become great at the game. I couldn't swim out. I was on the wrong end of the gun, if you know what I mean. Your uncle stepped in and vowed to make up for my debt, but he couldn't do it before he died."

"What! My Uncle Reggie really was a Spikes player?"

"The best at it too! I didn't want him to take my debt, but he insisted." I don't know if I should be angry or sad. Right now, it is just shock.

"I never got the real reason he died. No one has told me. It's becoming clearer now."

"Hey, D, we don't know if they offed him or not. That's speculation." Sedrick's company savior tone uncages my emotions.

"You serious, Sedrick. This is as much on you as anybody. My uncle would still be alive if it wasn't for you. You kept that from me this whole time! Why? Let me guess, it's my turn now. Did you set me up?"

"I didn't set you up, D. Although I come back, I don't win enough. I knew how good you were. How competitive you are. I knew you would excel at this, and look at you! You are becoming a favorite to win this tournament. Your odds are high man."

"I can't believe you. Why not tell me everything from the beginning? Would I have been pissed? Yes. But at least I would have known. You didn't have to pretend like you were trying to get me out of the house. This has been your play the whole time. None of what you have done has been for me."

"Was I looking out for my best interest? Yes…but at the same time, I was trying to set you up too."

"Stop with the lies, Sedrick!"

"I'm not lying! You weren't going anywhere with the warehouse job. I'm surprised you are still holding on to it. Everything that I thought about you is true and is coming true. I was wrong to shield you from all of this, but I'm not perfect. Listen, you win this tournament, and all of our troubles are over. Both of our lives are in the clear."

"My uncle died because of this game and now both of us are in the same position. What else have you discussed with him?"

"I know its bad, man. I know it is, but I'll tell you this. He will grant you *and* me, for that matter, a pardon…if you win the tournament! That means, no more debt, no more looking over your shoulder. We would be good. Then we could focus on taking this game to new heights."

"I don't think so, Sed. I win this thing, I'm done."

"I'm sorry, bro. It's not that simple. Don't you see what is going on here? They aren't going to just let you out. Why would they do that? So you could tear down this whole organization? Haven, aka Wine, was talking that mess and look where he is now. Still getting money!"

"Nah, Sed. I'm done with everything after this. I'm leaving. I'm done with this city, this game, and I'm definitely done with you. I'll do this on my own from here on out. Don't call me, don't text me, just keep your distance."

"C'mon, D. What has happened is on me, but you need me to navigate these swamps, man. There are traps everywhere trying to take advantage of guys like you."

"It's time I took a good friend's advice and not worry about the trouble I face and just focus on myself. I'll see you at the tournament, Sedrick, I suggest you be ready. You have a lot to play for."

"Okay, okay, if that's how you want it." Sedrick's attitude shifts to agitation. "I can't wait to see how you do when you don't know your opponent. When you don't have that little bit of an edge that takes you over the top."

Sedrick leaves and it felt different this time. A violation of trust is one thing for a thought-of best friend to do. He was willing to put my life in danger and had no intentions of informing me about it. There is an ill-fitted irony that bubbles deep. My best friend was the first one to lift my spirits after my uncle's death and was the one that put me in a situation where my life could be in jeopardy.

So this is how it feels. The emotion is back. That feeling I had at the reception after my uncle's death is back. I have never felt so alone. I don't even want to think about Sedrick right now, knowing it would be regretful thoughts. My mom definitely can't be told that her son could be on the chopping block and her faux-boyfriend is the maestro. I never got Hyung's number. I have always been independent but have never felt alone. I feel myself succumbing to the lights suspending from the dining room ceiling serving the role of hypnotist. I can't let myself do this right now. Rising from the ashes in my brain, I know a stroke of entertainment will provide me a powerful dose of endorphins to get me through this.

Shaking off these clothes and now, I can start thinking of what the night will bring! While it is time to rinse these thoughts away in the shower, I always forget that mom does laundry on this day and always washes my towel. There is a small napkin on the floor. I don't remember grabbing anything when I was out. It's Liz's number. This can't be a coincidence. A lonely guy now finds a person he hardly knows number when he was deciding to have some fun. I wish it was Camila's number. Well, Liz wanted to tell me something, anyway. Something about the tournament that I need to know. That is the last thing I want to hear. Maybe, I can just convince her to come out with me. No strings. Just fun, to get our minds off things.

"Hi, Liz?"

"Who is this?"

"Darren, you don't know my voice already?"

"No." That was not the answer I was expecting.

"Well, okay then. This was a bad idea…"

"No, wait. I'm sorry. I was just busy doing something, didn't mean to snap at cha. Soo, hi, what's up?"

"I know you told me to call you when I want to know about the tournament. It's not about that. I do want to know, but not now… Look, I have had a pretty sorry end of my day. You want to meet up somewhere? I'm not trying to date you, I'm not interested like that, we can just hang out and enjoy the night. Unless you're busy?"

"Hmmm, I'm actually bored as hell right now! House chores are no fun. Sure, sounds like fun. Where do you want to meet?"

"I'll text it to you. Thanks, Liz. You are actually doing me a favor."

"No problem, and hey, don't try anything you will regret. I'm involved." Liz says.

"I truly wasn't even thinking about it Liz. Just some camaraderie amongst peers if you know what I mean."

"Sounds like someone really wants to know about that tournament."

"Actually, I don't."

"It's fine, I can't wait to tell you all about it. See you soon!"

The feeling of regret immediately sets in. The last thing I want is to talk about Spikes for half the night. If I wanted pain, I would just sit at home and watch town hall videos. Sounds like Liz could use the night out too. She probably doesn't want to drown the night by talking about Spikes either.

Chapter 15

BEGINNING OF THE END

I'm glad I'm here. Liz keeps things light and is funny as heck. Maybe part of it has to do with what I'm consuming. It's a good energy in this place. The smell of beer and food is undeniable and expected. They really work to keep this place clean even as the night gets older and the temperaments begin to change. Liz asked me not to leave her alone because she doesn't feel like being approached tonight. She does not lack confidence. Outside of a bathroom break, I have held my end of the bargain. Usually nights like these have their own regrets, and this one is going to be no different. I thought that I shouldn't have started a tab. I might as well have told the bartender I didn't plan on walking straight later. If that's the way it ends up, so be it. I need this night.

"So are you going to eat that last stick?" Liz has been eyeballing this cheese stick for an unsettling long time. She has already had two more than I have.

"Yes, Liz. I'm eating that cheese stick." I have no shame. Dang it, I like cheese sticks too!

"Maybe you should order some more, I'll pay this time." I wonder if she really meant that she would pay or was that a test of how liberal I was going to be tonight.

"How about we order some real food…hamburger fries or something?" A separate artery clogging item would suit me better. I'm having the urge for greasy delights.

"Oh yeah, now you're talking! I like their hamburger fries. Soo, how you feeling?"

"Better than a few hours ago for sure! I'm glad you came; this has been fun." Surprisingly, lots of fun. Apparently I have been stressed and haven't even realized it. I just need to not think about it all and give my brain a break. Although I know one person in this bar, it feels good just to be around people that are just looking to enjoy themselves.

"It has been fun." Liz scrunches her face. Her mind minions are at work as she prepares to choose her next words. I can see it. "I get out a lot, don't get me wrong, but I really have had fun with you."

Now I'm worried about her next words. Is Liz attractive? Sure, but there is something about Camila. As weird as it seems to think about this, it would feel like I am cheating if I did anything with anyone else. At least, until I find out if she is interested in me. By Liz not responding quickly, I need to get out in front of this to squelch any further thoughts.

"Well, if you want this night to get spicier, I know a tabletop gaming place that is just getting things started." I think that should temper things a little.

"Sounds awesome, count me in!" Consider that attempt a fail.

"I was kidding, Liz. I don't play tabletop games."

"Oh, got it. So you were trying to use tabletop gaming as a joke. As if people who play those are lower…geeks, nerds, virgins, all the former stereotypical stuff."

"Kind of, but no. I was trying to make a joke, but I'm not the biggest fan of labels."

"What about tags?" Liz states with clear intent. I just set myself up for that. An attempt to deflect is in order.

"Like clothes tags, graffiti on the wall, where you going with that?" I'll see where she steers this ship and decide whether or not I'm going overboard.

"You know, the game tags."

Overboard it is. "I don't want to talk about that, Liz. That's a primary reason why we are out right now."

"You can't just avoid a dragon and hope it goes away. You have to slay it! Isolating yourself from the issue doesn't help it go away."

Suddenly the fun is sucked out of the room. This fun-loving person turned into teacher, and I turned into a disinterested student. No matter if Liz speaks truth or not, I'm not willing to listen to it and therefore the message will be lost on me.

"I hear ya, but ever since Sedrick persuaded me toward this game, things have gone from okay to worse. I should have known that there was no quick and easy fix out of a situation. I missed the signs. I have been an emotional tornado ever since I lost someone close to me. Then I find out what he was a part of...I don't want to reconcile that this is happening. I'm...I'm...I just need to win this tournament."

"Okay, bud. Let's just get out of here and go for a quick walk." Liz *must* be drunk to offer up going for a walk this late.

"This late...why would I want to invite trouble walking around this late?"

"I know a safe place, just stick with me."

Standing was a slight challenge, but I gather my things and follow Liz out the door.

"How far is this place?"

"A couple blocks over. We'll be there in no time."

The quiet in the air was more nerve wracking than soothing. My inebriated state is not helping with my discomfort.

"So, who did you lose that affected you this way? A parent—a sister or a brother?"

I can't escape the grasp of my vulnerability. I want to tell her but I shouldn't. Don't say anything, don't say anything.

"My uncle. Look, Liz, please don't repeat anything I'm about to tell you. You have to promise me."

"I promise...wait! This doesn't have anything to do with mass murder...if it does, I'm out."

"No, but it seems a little shady. So, I heard my uncle was a legend at Spikes. You probably heard of him. His name was Fireball."

"Fireball was your uncle? Seriously? This game is getting smaller."

"Yes, he was. And now, I have managed to take on his debts. If I don't win, I'm beginning to think I may lose more than the match."

"Why would you think that? I mean, your sponsor won't be happy with you since you have this entire positive momentum thing going, but besides that you have nothing to worry about."

"This is what happens when games like this are underground. As they grow, vendettas form and more money changes hands. The more money, the more anxiety. That anxiety turns into the people of power letting everyone else know who is in charge by whatever means necessary."

"Darren, you can't live based off of speculation, but I might be able to help you—if you are interested."

"How?"

"I've been undercover investigating the construct of this game. You just provided me what I needed and that is someone close enough to the head of the snake that I can chop it off." Liz's words temporarily petrify me. Escaping the situation is the first option.

"This conversation is over."

"You wish it was, don't you? I already have shots of you talking with me. Knowing how cutthroat Spikes is, you really don't want those pictures to get into the wrong hands."

"Ain't this some mess. I don't need this right now, Liz…if that's your name! This isn't what I want."

"You should have thought about that before you decided to dive head first into this game. These are the types of consequences that occur when people either don't think, don't care, or think they can get away with it. No matter how you look at it, you fall in one of those categories. So which one is it for you, Darren? Hmm, you know Uncle Sam always wants his proper cut, and you are getting way more cash handed to you than is on *the books*. You even quit your tax paying job for this, so I know you were trying to take this as far as you could. The good news is this doesn't have to be the end. It is a beginning to a new beginning only if you decide to help me put an end to Spikes. Oh, and let's just stick with Liz or Elizabeth for now."

The worse possible situation has arisen, and I put myself in it. I can't tell if I'm breathing, so I'm going to take a moment. What will I do once this is over? Camila and her family would be exposed. Maybe there is a way out. A way I can have this work in my favor.

"Okay, Liz, if I help you I need some assurances."

"I expected as such, what do you have in mind?"

"I need you to help Camila's family become American citizens."

"Can't do that. Maybe some working visas. Don't get your hopes up on that either. You know, Darren, if I was Camila, I wouldn't be too happy with you. You just outed her family to a federal agent. You pretty much told me to get ICE involved in this. I understand you are under a lot of stress, but you are not in the best bargaining position."

Control is a myth produced and reproduced by those that believe in power and hierarchy. Nations are built on this premise. Couple that with religion and laws produced by those with "control" and what you get is a largely obedient society. Those with control relish it and those without, do without it with the understanding that the promise land is beyond the flesh they currently sit in. An honorable life is the primary goal over control. Although the carrot of control is still dangled, it primarily serves as a rocking chair. We indulge in the consistent movement, but realistically we are going nowhere. My life is now at a crossroads. I have been stripped of any idea that I'm in control. All that is left are my beliefs.

"Darren, if you are still in that brain of yours, I'm going to need a decision."

My blank stare masks my thoughts as I need to cease motor functions for cerebral analysis. It has provided me an opportunity to reflect. This reflection has allowed me to come up with a way I can get out of this thing.

"Sorry, it was just a lot to process."

"I understand that, but just know that what I am asking you to do is the right thing. No one is perfect in this life, not even those willing to provide law and order. When there is a chance to right wrongs, we must take it. That is what you can do, right now!"

"And that is what I intend to do. Do you realize that there are people involved in this game that are being held hostage by those that are supporting them? It's true! Camila is one of them. Deportation of her family members has been placed over her head. A promise of citizenship as long as she puts up with their BS! I am not for people remaining in this country illegally; however, I am a proponent of those that are contributing to society and pursuing a dream. There are citizens of this country that do far worse things. I say that to say this, for my help in bringing down Spikes, all I ask is you leave Camila's family alone and let them have an opportunity in this coun-try...*and* I get off without any jail time."

"I will see what I can do. You do realize what you are asking me to do goes against my principles, my beliefs, and the law to help someone that made the conscious decision to do something they know is illegal."

"I was wrong, I realize that. I have been swimming upstream ever since this game was introduced in my life. But I kept swimming, because I believed in a light at the end of this. A road to legitimacy for the game. I started to believe that. I still do. Just tell me what you need me to do."

"Just keep winning. You told me that you needed to win this tournament. If you win this tournament and can produce a meeting with the head of Spikes, I will do everything in my power to ensure you have no jail time."

"What about Camila's family?"

"I will do what I can for them too. You have my word, and that is the best collateral you are going to get."

Could I push for a better deal? Probably not. Now it's time to close the deal. In the end, this could be a proper end to it all. It would be an unsettling justice to close this chapter for my uncle and myself.

"Okay, it's done then. This doesn't change how I feel about you right now. I'll play my role and win this tournament. Then be done with your sorry tail."

"Just remember, I didn't get you started with Spikes. I didn't try to hone your skills while having my own ulterior motive. You need to channel that energy elsewhere. I'll check in on you from time to time. Make sure you answer. *I really had fun tonight... See you at the tournament!*"

Hearing her go from federal agent to Suds with those final words pissed me off, and she knew it. She also knows there is not much I can do but comply and turn this situation into lemonade.

Chapter 16

WHERE THE HEART IS

(In Spanish)

"Camila!"

"Yes, Grandma."

"Go help your mother with dinner."

"I'm almost done sewing Sabrina's dress, and then I will be right in there, Grandma."

"You can finish the dress later. Your mother needs you now."

"Yes, Grandma."

(End Spanish)

Camila fervently walks over and immediately scrubs in. This is how Camila's days go—caring for family in any way she knows how. There was too much to get done. No time for a petty argument that leads to a recant and an eventual resolution. Loving by showing her family how much she cares will do more than any words she speaks.

She has worked hard for their house. It sits as a modest three-bedroom home. The first home the family has ever owned, and she paid for it. Although not a fan of what she has done to make the money, she has no thought of atonement for the results. Resolute in her goal, she pushes pass any fatigue and frustration that comes from sponsor demands and family commitments. Visits from her two aunts and one uncle help. Mostly, it is the warm smile from her little sister

Sabrina that serves as the anesthesia to the surgery life is performing on her. For now, the focus is dinner.

(In Spanish)

"Prepare the tortillas, Sabrina, and I will do the rest," Mariana, Camila's mom, warmly says.

"Is this your way of giving me a night off?"

"There are never any days or nights off. There are just days where more is required and days where we make the decision to do less."

(English)

"Mom, you are so wise. You could have done so many things. Why come here and deal with what we do? Feel unwanted at times."

"I have done many things, and the most important thing was caring for you and your sister. I learned long ago that you can't depend on anyone for your happiness. My family is the most important thing in my life, and I am so happy to see you share that same passion."

"But loving family doesn't make money, Mom. It doesn't sustain life. Dad is always at work, and he makes very little. I don't know how you do it."

"Camila." Mariana glowingly looks at Camila. "I have learned so much from your *abuela*. You know the best advice your grand-mother gave me?"

Camila's body relaxes as she readies for the words. Her eyes connect with her mother's as she embraces the moment.

"Let your mind do the thinking, but let your heart guide you. Your *abuela* did not want me to live life like a leaf in the wind. She knew if I followed my heart, no matter what happened, I would be happy or accepting of the results. That is the way I have lived, and I could not be happier."

Mariana kisses Camila and absorbs her with adulation.

"Now, let's get back to work, or we are going to have your father in the kitchen with us, and we both don't want that."

The joyous sound that followed echoed throughout the kitchen and living room. Sabrina even snickered at her mother's known disdain for her husband's kitchen fails. They continued to work on dinner with playful exchanges and light spirits. They unexpectedly hear the door opening, putting the entire house into mannequin mode.

The tearful gentleman drudges through the door and drops his jacket on the floor. Without words being spoken, Mariana wipes her hands, gracefully touches Camila's hand, and embraces her husband.

"They let me go, Mariana. I'm sorry…I'm sorry, but I'm going out in the morning. A couple of the guys told me a few locations I can go to find quick work."

"I'm not worried, and there is no need for you to apologize. You are doing your best. Just remember the blessings that we have. Things will work out for us. Food is almost ready. Wash up and come eat."

"I'm really not that hungry, dear. I think I'm going to shower and go to bed. Would you mind saving me some for later?"

"Of course."

As Camila's father sloths to the bedroom, Mariana and Camila begin finishing up dinner. Camila tries to wait for her mother to break the silence, but as minutes go by she feels the elephant getting bigger.

"Mom, you know it's okay. I will take care of us. I only have one more of these tournaments left, and when I win, they promised me they would take care of you, dad, and grandma."

"Your father and I's burden will never be placed on our child. We know you bring in the most money, but as long as your father is working, he feels right with it all. We want better for you, and you are getting better. The time you have is your own, and promise me, that once this is over you stop worrying so much about us."

"But you said go with your heart."

"And I mean that. I don't want you living out your days taking care of us. You need to live Camila! See and experience things. Both you and Sabrina have an opportunity to push the family forward. You can't do that in this house…with us."

"I can, Mom, and I will. I love you! I'm not going anywhere. I will make sure I can buy a house big enough that you won't know whether I'm home or out. Me and my boyfriend will have all the peace and quiet in the world."

"Boyfriend? Who is this boyfriend?"

"Not literally, Mom!"

"There something you are not telling me. There is someone that is causing you to consider love. It's okay, I like it. You are living! That's what I dream!"

"It really is nothing Mom, no boyfriend. I am dreaming, and we share this dream together."

Minus Camila's father, the family dinner continues on. There was laughter and words of wisdom. The succulent meal did not take place without a cloud over it. The empty chair beside Mariana was a noted reminder that things are not the same today as they were the day before.

All members were assisting with the cleaning. Each detail had an owner and Camila was leading the charge to take on her father's normal contribution. As they approached the end of cleanup, Camila muted the cleanup music.

"I'm going to head out, Mom. I want to get some practice rounds in. This tournament means too much for me not to be sharp."

"So, it sounds like you won't be letting anyone win this time."

"Those days are over!"

Camila ventures out to one of her favorite pool halls. She was not alone in that sentiment. Many enjoyed the tables. Her peace and quiet was quickly interrupted.

"Wasup, Camila!"

Camila looked up as if her look alone could make the person go away. Her face softens as she recognizes who it is, but not by much.

"Hi, Sedrick."

"I can always tell when the tournament is getting closer because I see more and more of my people in here, if you know what I'm saying. I'm happy I ran into you here, because I have a proposition."

"Not interested."

"Thanks for listening, dang! C'mon, let's get serious…"

"I just told you I'm not interested. What's the problem?" Camila is not smothering her tension anymore.

"The problem is you stand to win a lot of money if you listen to me and not as much if you don't."

Camila did not think the words that were still bakery fresh would be challenged so soon. Her mom's voice is in her head. Her heart is telling her to not trust Sedrick and continue in this tournament without any additional baggage or concerns from other players. Her mind tells her to listen because she needs as much money as she can especially with her father out of work. Time to make a choice.

"I'm listening."

As Camila dissects Sedrick's reaction, a slight pain creeps across her stomach and then stops to linger. Her skin was feeling as if it was sliding off her bones. She is faced with a moral paradox. A battle she is fighting within while dealing with an outer one.

"I knew you had it in you. Listen, there is an opportunity here for us both to get paid in this tournament. I will be the first to tell you that I need money desperately, but I'm not afraid to say you are better than me. So I was thinking. I have an in on the sponsor-driven betting pool. We can place a wager on us being in the top four, the final, or even one of us winning. I'm thinking if we bet on the final, that will be a good bet, but it doesn't bring in the big money we could get if we put it all on one of us winning. The odds are low for me so it's a bigger pay out. The odds are a little higher for you, but it is still lucrative."

"I can't remember the last tournament you won, Sedrick! I know what I'm capable of, and unfortunately for you, I know your ceiling as well."

"What you don't know is all the behind the scenes strings that I pull. You think this is my first time? It's a reason I'm still in this game even with my losses. I'm a strong ally to have, and I can assure you, this tournament, you will get my best. I can't say the same about before. I won't even put it on me winning! I'll put it on you...if you're with me."

"I need to think about it." Camila looks away and plays a shot on the table.

"Bet needs to be placed within the next few days. I'll give you two days. Imagine being able to win the tournament and get over a million dollars but also win a bet and win a couple million dollars. We could leave this game and have time to start a different life!"

"I'll think about it."

"Here's a phone. There is only one programmed number in it. If I don't hear from you in two days, I will have someone else ready to take the deal you didn't…"

"Your friend, Darren?" Camila wants Sedrick to know that she has an idea of what is going on as well.

"Let's just say, it will be someone just as capable of winning this tournament as you are. I'm coming to you first for a reason. Call me."

Sedrick grabs a cue and caroms a shot off the rails knocking in two solids.

"It's a different game now."

"It was stripes shot, by the way!" Camila curls her lip, annoyed by Sedrick's conversation with her.

Sedrick waves Camila off and leaves the building. For Camila, he hasn't left yet. She can't dismiss his words and the financial implication it could have on her family. She is not a gambler by nature, but her belief in herself makes this a possible proposition. With that amount of money, she could leave Spikes. Another option also presents itself, she could afford to avoid any future troubles with her family and leave the country. It is a consideration she needs to and will take seriously.

Chapter 17

DEBRIEF

Banks stands in front of her colleagues, absorbing the positive comments as she prepares to hit them with the scale-tipping information that she believes will crumble Spikes.

"Very impressive work, Banks! To pull this off in two years proves one of two things: the fragile structure of their operation, or your ability to analyze and probe the links necessary to break a case wide open," The Director praises.

Whiteside interjects while looking at Banks with a coiled tongue, "I'd go with the former, boss. No offense, Banks. You did good work, no doubt…but this is amateur hour. Whenever you involve young adults in prominent positions, things are bound to go wrong sooner, rather than later. I'm happy for you, though. To get one of those impressionable minds to flip and *potentially* get you the big dog, that's high-level agent work right there."

The Director looks on unamused by the child that has taken over for her decorated agent. Diffusion rests at the front of her mind.

"You done, Whiteside?" the Director scolds.

Banks is not going to let the Director feel the need to step in on her account. Dealing with people like Whiteside is easy work for her. She stands up a little straighter ready to respond, as if the Director didn't intervene.

"Maybe once I'm done, Whiteside, I'll help you close your case. I heard you could use a mentor with your interview strategies. I know how you might feel when others look at you thinking you are dragging your feet or just struggling to make up ground. Either way, it looks bad. You know where to find me; just let me know."

"Ease up, Banks, I was giving you a compliment. Am I the only one that gets the icebox?"

The Director conceals a smile while others openly dig Whiteside for his superfluous statement. Amanda Banks remains unfazed.

"Now, if you are done with being condescending instead of supporting a fellow agent, I haven't even disclosed the best part of all of this. My source's life is being threatened. I aim to substantiate these claims to add a litany of additional charges against the target."

"Did you tell your source he was going to be the cheese in the trap?" Whiteside takes another stab at tripping up Banks.

"He understands the risk, Whiteside."

The Director has primarily been a silent contributor. She has always been adept at mental Jenga. She attacks omission and perceived misdirection as deceit. She values her time, which promotes little patience when a brief meanders on the fringes.

"I'm still wrapping my head around this, Banks. What would get your source to turn on the target like this? There has to be something you offered." The Director's inquisition fortifies Banks. Banks knows she needs to be quick and straightforward.

"Freedom."

"C'mon, Amanda. I was on your side, and now we have to go through twenty questions. We all know that's never enough." The Director continues probing Banks.

"Yes, ma'am. You are right."

Soft chuckles fill the room like an unclaimed fart in a quiet middle school class room.

Amanda states the obvious. "I told my source he would only get a year, maybe two at most, for his part in this. I couldn't get a commitment. I asked him what it would take, and he told me."

Amanda has the weight of everyone's eyes on her lips. She knew judgement would rain down on her. This is the most important case she has had and is motivated to not waste this opportunity. She proceeds cautiously, but undeterred.

"I said that I would do what I can to help the source's illegal immigrant family, become legal and not be deported."

"So you lied to your source! Not the best tactic but one I could understand given your position, case, and what appears to be desperation to make headway," the Director sarcastically empathizes.

Amanda's now hazy gaze paces the audience. When she pursued this job, she knew there would be days like this. Her mother told her. Her uncle told her. There would be a time when her convictions would be tested by a higher authority, and she would have to make a decision. Not a decision that you have time to collect your thoughts about; it would be in the moment. The Director's challenge has introduced this moment.

"I'm sorry, ma'am, but that's not true. I did not lie to my source. I intend to follow through."

"Who is going to sign off on this, exactly, Dr. Seuss? You made an empty promise. You better hope they have younger kids that they brought here, and then maybe you could entertain submitting a DACA application for them. Even that is not guaranteed."

"Ma'am, I really need your support on this. This is our department's best chance to close this case in years! Who knows when we will have another opening? All I need is your help."

"You will always have my support, within reason. This is not a debate. Attaining legal citizenship is not our dominion, find a new angle if you must, but drop that idea from your thought process."

As Amanda turns to the crowd of colleagues, she was unable to chase anyone's eyes into compassion or agreement. The briefing has now taken on another tone. She fiddles through a few papers prior to continuing her brief, all the while wishing it was over. A milestone-moment-turned-setback was not going to wreck her confidence in finalizing this case. She wraps up the brief and steps away from the firing squad. The fact is, she has her source. That will take her to the organizer of Spikes. For the big picture, nothing has changed. Though she feels this may be more difficult to navigate than what she first thought. She mulls over hedging expectations.

"You wasted no time calling me." Darren's incredulous tone attempts to set the bounds for the conversation.

"We need to meet."

"Now? I can't...I'm running a few errands for my mom. We'll have to do it another time."

"If you even want a shot at saving your friend's family, you will meet me."

"I'm done with this conversation...*Liz*. As a matter of fact, I might be done with this whole deal altogether."

"That's a bad thought. You would rather go to jail, see your friend's family deported, and the pain on your mother's face when she has to visit you? What would be worse is that you could have avoided all of it. You don't want that on your conscience for years."

Darren's pause provides all the data she needs. He begins contemplating the scenario...or thinking of a new way out.

"How 'bout this. Finish your errands, and let's meet at Quaint. Best curly cheese fries you will ever have. I'll buy, you listen. I did discuss the issue with my boss today; you will want to hear what I have to say."

Darren surrenders under the weight of his lack of leverage. "Okay, I'll meet you there at six."

* * *

Banks' mind acquiesces to the last meeting between the two. It was meant to be fun, a getaway. At least that is what she believes he was thinking. This case could be the punchline or rocket fuel for her career, and it started with her casual meeting with Darren...as Suds. Amanda has not become numb to her task. No matter how much training she has or simulations she goes through. She remembers the looks in her suspect's eyes when they realize all they thought they knew about her was a lie. Her suspects become artists in that moment. She watches them paint a picture through her face—her soul as the canvas. It is a look that represents a lesser being. An oxymoronic mental exchange occurs. She knows she is an arbiter for justice. In most cases, this will require a measure of suffering and venom. A realization uncomfortably pours over her. Her soul is not healing as fast as she expected. However, she is not paid to adhere to her personal feelings. There is a tangible threat to our societal norms that requires her attention. In her lens, the bigger picture clears the mind. A needed cleansing as her suspect arrives.

"How is tournament prep coming, Darren?"

"No...uh, uh. You don't get to go there. I'm not here for the person I thought I was getting to know. I'm here for the person in front of me. The real you! Why do you need me anyway?"

"It's my job to check up on my suspects, and in your case, witness. I don't love putting people through this as much as you enjoy going through it, but I do *love* getting justice. I do *love* catching people and putting them behind bars when they thought the laws of this country was not good enough for them. I have a hunger for that, and I'm not apologizing for it. You are not innocent in this, Darren, as much as you try to make it out to be."

"I don't want to have anything more to do with you, Liz. I put myself here; you're right. Just understand, my intentions were good. I never hurt anyone. I am trying to grind and make a living like millions of other people. I had a skill that I was able to offer for a short period of time and went for it. I don't know many people that would have resisted this, if they were in my position. But wait, I can't expect you to understand. The rules and the regulations definitively cover every scenario including those that embrace nuance. Our laws are reactionary. People are punished before our country realizes that the situation wasn't as bad as they thought or they were just wrong. That will be the case with Spikes. You will look back at this a decade from now and regret the side that you were on. I will let you know clearly and for the last time before the tournament, that I'm fine. I will uphold my bargain. You make sure you uphold yours. I'm outta here, Liz."

Darren begins to get up, and Amanda addresses the attempted angry exit.

"Darren! Our laws are not perfect, but neither are we. If we don't have order, we have chaos. I'm not here to convince you. This is the way it is. And truly, you knew this before making your decision.

My advice, own this Darren…I will uphold my end of the bargain. After the tournament, we will talk."

Darren rises, throws a few dollars on the table for the drink, and exits Quaint. A conversation like this doesn't lend itself to an appetite. Amanda did not expect a cordial encounter; however, she did want to unite the cause in spite of their differences. Unfortunately, the divide was only widening. After paying the bill, she readies herself and exits. As she walks to her car, Amanda is resigned to the fact that once the bridge of reveal is crossed, it crumbles. Emotions cause waves of action. She does not allow herself to be overtaken by them, because justice can ill-afford that.

Chapter 18

MONEY POT

The building lights up the dark sky as the wealthy trickle in for the annual art festival. Smooth jazz and light chatter fills the enormous foyer while the mixed smells of fragrance and hors d'oeuvres remind the guests of the company they keep. With over 15,000 works in multiple departments and 235,000 objects and displays, Mark Finney and his business partners endeavored to pattern their ambitious creation after the famous Louvre. While the ambiance swells with class, this night reeks of multi-purpose. After schmoosing and acknowledging the social ladder of guests, Finney makes his way to a closed-off wing of his wonder palace. The area is understood to be under construction as he aims to grow his eclectic collection. Guarded by armed security and enough cameras to watch over a subdivision, Finney greets and moves through the halls. He stops momentarily to gaze upon a piece in his future prehistoric archaeological department that ties past and present. A settling smile graces his face as Finney takes a moment to soak in what has been accomplished while basking in what is to come. Finney does not act upon any feat without precision thought. This night was no different. It requires successfully striking the balance to fulfill the desires of class and the insatiable tendencies of his constituents. Now staring at the grandiose entrance, subdued conversation can be heard just beyond the doors. He chooses not to enter and heads down the hall where he enters a large conference room. All the Spikes sponsors eagerly greet him as he enters. What they do not know is that Finney means to promulgate the direction of Spikes.

"It's like an act of congress to get you all in one room…but this is a night that we will all remember. The closure of one chapter and the beginning of the next."

Necks begin to turn as they look upon each other for answers. They soon understand that only one person knew what was going to happen and that was Mark Finney.

This is a night where lots of money will be made by a couple of them so it is not a playful feeling in the room. Myron Campbell is quick to point that out to Finney. "Mark, I think I can speak for everyone here when I say, tell us what the hell is going on?"

"Our patience has been rewarded. I have been gauging the interest across the country on creating a professional Spikes league. I want it to be more than just tournaments where you see the same players. There will be teams that challenge each other on a weekly basis in locations across the country. I have collected the money. I have the analytics and surveys to prove its success. I have donors. What I need are owners. That is where you come in. I want you all to own a franchise. You have been very loyal to me and this cause. It is time we take the next step. Legitimacy!"

"And taxes," One of the sponsors cries out.

Another sponsor speaks with his native accent, "I'm a little worried that this will become an American sport. That takes away from any international appeal. I am in this for the money. I don't see how this benefits my bottom line, but I am intrigued."

"Guys and gals, I need for you to continue to trust me. I have gotten us this far, and now I'm steering this ship right into the treasure. This will be international, and I will explain everything in detail. I will ensure you will all get a packet of the league details, the by-laws, and most importantly, what you stand to gain from this. What I need now is your trust. Are you in?"

Finney and the group of sponsors excitedly exit the room and prepare for the scintillation of another event. The massive doors open to reveal the setup. There are multiple bars embedded in the deep corners of the spacious hall. Billiard tables are set up to accommodate small audiences around them with one table, with white felt and a logo located near the front by a makeshift stage and podium that will be used for the finals. A theater-sized projection screen displays the thirty-two-person tournament layout. This is the largest Spikes tournament ever assembled and seemingly the last in its current format.

* * *

Camila stares at the group entering the room but is laser-focused on her sponsor. She allows herself a moment of anger before contemplating the offer Sedrick made. She thinks back to the phone conversation she had with Sedrick and if she made the right choice. No matter what, she needs to win. If she wins, it doesn't matter. She heads to the restroom for some quiet and prayer before the tournament begins. She knows her pre-tourney process needs to be sped up so she focuses on her first opponent. Should be a win, but it won't be easy if her mind is not right. Camila slides her glove on and wonders the future for her and her family. The positive feeling she has is that no matter what happens in this game, this is the end. She doesn't plan on competing in one more Spikes tournament no matter what her sponsor says. Even if it takes leaving the country with them, she is willing to do what it takes so they are safe.

* * *

Sedrick sees Camila exiting the bathroom and provides a smile and a wave. He receives nothing in return. He chalks it up to Camila just being Camila before the tournament, nothing new. Sedrick checks his watch and looks at the tournament setup. How it stands now, he would have a chance to meet Camila in the final, but would have to go through his friend, Darren to get there. The larger than normal gaggle of nonplayers and sponsors in the room makes him wonder how in the world they have kept Spikes underground this long. Money and power is truly a strong motivator. He looks over and sees Suds having her drink before the tournament and sees Darren talking to her. He figured it was time to make his presence felt.

"Hey, you two." Darren suppresses his feelings by taking a sip of a drink. "Oh, you giving me the silent treatment now? I'm surprised you are over here with Suds. I thought you might be talking to Camila. You turning into Haven now, my man!"

"I can talk to whoever I want, Sed; don't read into things. I wanted a drink; Suds is always drinking before the games pop off, so I decided to join her. This is the biggest moneymaker of our lives, excuse me if I need a drink."

"No, problem, bro…I get it, just strange because you have been distant recently."

"I think you know why, Sed."

Sedrick looks at Suds who in turn looks away before returning to listening.

"Do you two have something to work out before we get started? I can leave; it won't take me any time to finish this," Suds hurriedly states.

"Nah, you cool, Suds. I think we done talking. But, hey, look up at the bracket. I get you in the second round so I hope your buzz wears off by then or it won't last long," Sedrick sharply fires at Suds.

"Maybe I'm doing this to give you a chance," Suds quips with a raised eyebrow.

Sedrick rolls his head and eyes and steps in. "Yeah, yeah, sure, Suds. Hey, D, did you notice who is here?"

Darren does a quick scan over the room but doesn't see anyone out of the ordinary.

"It's the man from Bushleague."

He sees the back of a figure walking away in the general direction where Sedrick was looking. "That's the Spikes organizer?"

Suds' attention immediately turns to identify who they are speaking of, but he was out of sight before she laid eyes on him.

"Where did he go?" Suds excitedly indulges.

"You so nosey, Suds. This conversation is between me and Lock."

"Whatever, I don't care anyway. Good luck, Lock. I can't wait to face you later," Suds responds. "I'm going to love seeing your face when you realize how pissed your sponsor will be after you lose to me. It's going to make my day."

Suds nauseatingly walks away and the preparation for the tournament concludes. Officials are beginning to take their positions and the countdown is down to five minutes. It is time for the players to take their positions and sponsors to align with their players.

"Remember the deal, D…It's still on the table for you. The unfortunate thing is we are in the same bracket, but if you win, it's set up for a large amount of money coming our way…if you did what I asked you to do."

"I always bet on myself, so that's done. I noticed Haven in my bracket as the 1-seed and I'm the 2-seed. I thought you said Haven wasn't the best player."

Sedrick smiles. "He's up there. Well, it's my time to shine, bro. Good luck to you, D."

"Yeah, man. Good luck."

Darren's face subdues the resentment in his heart. His Spikes name is getting a workout after dealing with both Suds and Boomerang before the tournament starts. He expels air as if no one in the room was there. It served as a needed reset for the task at hand. Lock was now ten wins away from freeing himself from his own entrapment. He has learned a lot from this experience, both good and bad. He pans the bracket to see his first round pairing and the location. He looks over the room and acknowledges the competition, Camila, and Sedrick, and now makes his way to his sponsor. Myron begins to clap as he approaches the table. Once he looks at Myron, he feels it happening. It is similar to a tingling in the body and a moment when everything becomes clear. As much as he would like to drop Myron where he stands, he has effectively blocked everything out and is now ready to finish this.

Spades peeks over at Lock's table and manages a brief smirk of a smile. She has seen that look and completely understands what that means. His first opponent does not stand a chance, and he will be difficult to beat if he can sustain that state for five rounds. Refocusing on her task, Spades has decided to break, and she pockets her first three balls. This was an optimum feel-good start to the tournament for her.

* * *

Sedrick makes quick work of his first round, winning 2–0. He stands at the end of the table, mockingly yawning, while he watches Suds in a tough match that is tied 1–1. Suds is not amused and says hello with one finger. Sedrick laughs it off. He looks across the room and makes eye contact with Darren who defeated his first round opponent easily. Darren's match also ended in a 2–0 advantage. Sedrick's playfulness turns to seriousness as he realizes Suds really could lose. He wants to be the one to take her out. Suds' opponent is down to one ball, while she has three. Suds knocks in the first ball clean setting up her second shot nicely. Sedrick fake sneezes really loud as Suds takes the shot. Normally, an official will let a situation like this slide; however, this official calls foul and demands a reset of the shot. He also orders Sedrick away, to Suds' delight. After her opponent missed the final shot, Suds delivers by sinking her opponent's cue ball to win the game and the match, 2–1. Suds looks at the competition and randomly sticks to the slickly-dressed Haven. Haven had just polished off his opponent, 2–0.

The first round ends and a brief five-minute intermission ensues. The competitors do not wander far from their tables as they prepare for the next round. The bracket updates, and the competitors take a look to see who they will be facing. Sedrick and Suds realize the winner of their match will potentially face Haven. The competitors look to make eye contact with their next opponent, except Haven. If Haven has ever been shaken, no one has seen it. Haven approaches Sedrick as the clock ticks down for his match with Suds.

"You nervous yet?" Haven smiles at Sedrick.

"You serious, Haven? You know me, I'm ready."

"I do know you, Boomerang, but there's no coming back from this. And it's *Wine*, not Haven, thank you, while we're amongst company. Just know, if you win, I won't take it easy on you."

Darren comes over and steps in.

"You can't avoid me anymore. My rematch is coming."

"I hope so... Lock, is it? I never avoided you; I just think it's better to have an audience to see me work."

* * *

While the tournament goes on, Mark Finney has since exited the area. He speaks to his head of security, seemingly receiving a report. Finney heads to the study area at the back of a future exhibit and unveils a vault. The vault contains an abundance of cash stacks, a couple of artifacts, and some precious metals. He opens a box that is comparable to the size of a safety deposit box and grabs a few documents before leaving. He continues the conversation with the guard as he seals the vault.

"There will be an opportunity when I will gather all of the contestants on the stage, step to the side and offer them a hand, which will be your cue. I need to make sure everyone that needs to exit the building can, do it appropriately and orderly. No matter what, I need for this to happen."

"Yes, sir. I have my people placed so the sponsors will be ushered one way, and everyone else will be taken care of. We just need everyone to be in a spot which makes it more conducive to exit," the guard answers orderly.

"They know where they need to be. Already covered. Thank you. I need to go check on our other guests. I'll return later."

* * *

Round 2 concludes with Spades, Wine, Boomerang, and Lock amongst four others advancing. Suds walks away frustrated and annoyed with her loss to Boomerang. Boomerang bows and laughs as she distances herself. Round 3 highlight matches has Boomerang facing Wine, Spades faces cowboy Bentley, and Lock faces Jewel. Suds watches the competitive games take place. She can feel the intensity heating up. Amanda knows the players in this game do not love what they are doing, but watching them fight for their living causes those unsettling feelings to rise to her emotional surface again. She steps out in the hallway to get away for a minute and is greeted immediately by security.

"Can we help you, ma'am?"

She takes note of four heavily armed guards standing there. She does not remember them being there earlier.

"Uh, just looking for the bathroom."

"Head back in, and you will see it. Would you like for me to show you?"

The guards look does not mirror the nicety of his words.

"No, no… Thank you. I'll find it."

Amanda begins to wonder why the area is so heavily guarded for such an esteemed group. She rationalizes that the money at stake is the highest ever. Possibly it could be the pristine location for the tournament. Something in her mind is giving her pause that it could be something more. She heads to the restroom and ensures her concealed weapon is loaded. Amanda understands the environment she is in. She trusts her instincts and until proven otherwise; she will not be a helpless victim.

She resurfaces to the playing floor, and she doesn't have to look at the score to know who is winning. Bentley is sweating it out against Spades, Lock and Jewel are both intensely focused, and Wine is smiling at Boomerang. Being out of the tournament has left her to focus on what is important. She decides to go speak with her sponsor to see if she is able to shake the tree.

"You had an early exit…again. I'm beginning to question your existence, in this game, that is," Amanda's sponsor quietly admonishes.

"At this level, it only takes one mistake to lose."

"True, but you made more than one and lost to a journeyman player at best. He is nothing more than a write in. Out of the thirty-two competitors, there are really only eight or nine legitimate top players, and out of those, only three or four could be considered amongst the best. I expected more from you. I expected a top four finish. This trend cannot continue, and it will not continue if you are to stay on payroll. I would hate to fire you, Elizabeth."

"It's not me you have to worry about. However, you should give some thought to the number of armed security outside this place. This is a nonviolent affair. There has never been a need for this much security. There have been large pots of money being distributed before. There have been other tournaments. Why the security now?"

"Why are you concerned with such things? This is a library and a museum with millions of dollars' worth of artifacts here. It must be protected. As for you, I would never put you in an unsafe position. You remember our deal. I take care of you, you take care of me... which you need to improve and soon."

"Armed guards is a reason for concern when it hasn't been the norm," Suds snipes back.

"Stop worrying, Elizabeth. This will all be over soon."

Amanda shrinks away from her sponsor, unsure now, more than before. She focuses her attention back towards the action, and she sees Lock bury a difficult shot to win the match against Jewel. The observers erupt in cheer as respect is shown between the competitors. We have now arrived to the final four contestants: Wine, Lock, Spades, and Purify. Amanda approaches to talk to Lock about her concerns.

"Lock, gotta sec?" Suds gestures at Lock.

Spades looks at Lock. Lock addresses Spades look with a quick nonverbal and then begins to follow Suds. Spades shakes her head in disapproval.

"Something's wrong here."

"Why are you doing this? I told you what I was willing to do. I told you I don't want to deal with you until after and yet you keep making things real awkward. Spades is thinking something I can tell. I never brought you up before. Why would I give a damn about anything going on outside of that table right now? My livelihood is on the line Liz...sorry, Suds. Dang, show some boundaries."

"Darren, this is not about us, and I promise you, I will clear up any misconception about us by the end of the night, but this is serious."

Darren removes his guard as Amanda prepares the flames for consumption.

"There is something large scale that is happening, and it's not good for anyone. There are armed guards collecting outside of those doors…"

Darren's head and face sags as his interest wanes.

Suds continues, "Since when do they have this many armed personnel, looking like a strike team for these events? I can tell you, never! It may be time to DQ yourself and get out of dodge; this isn't going to end well."

"Okay, stop. So you're asking me to bow out of a tournament that I need to win to recapture my life and instead, get disqualified and face not only you and the authorities, but even worse the fate of the Spikes gods? It sounds like you are trying to set me up for a fall. That's crazy. Liz! I'm not doing it. I have the biggest match of my career against the only person left that I'm not sure I can win against. I ain't got time for this, Liz. Why don't you see, I'm trying to do the right thing? I'm trying to get through this. Just let me get through this without constantly placing me in compromising positions. You are undercover, correct? Start acting like it and stop acting like you care about me or anyone else here. I know what you are about and you got me. I am 'owning it' as you mentioned before. I just want you and what you stand for out of my life! Now please, please, please, Liz, leave…me…alone for a couple hours."

Darren turns to head toward the semifinal tables.

"Word of advice, don't get involved with people you work with," Wine retorts as Darren walks by.

Wine's words deepen the wound. He doesn't know the situation and never will. Darren continues on to the table.

Round 4 is set to begin. Darren can't shake his last encounter with Haven. He remembers the confidence leaving his body as he grasped to retain it. Haven also remembers. He chalks his cue and smirks in Darren's direction. Darren conjures up an uncommitted scowl. Realizing his futile attempt, he breaks eye contact. Darren is not proud that he is envious of the confidence that Haven exudes. Haven is dressed exquisitely with his patented, custom designer suit and shoes. Fashion is not Darren's comfort zone, but he recognizes a good look when he sees it, and Haven looks the part. Darren shakes off his complimentary thoughts to focus on what could happen if he does not win and it is working. The officials start making their way over to the last two tables. Darren, now refocused on the task, nods his head up and down while surveying the colors of Haven's eyes. He wants him to know that this will be different than the last time they went against each other.

As the astutely dressed officials provide instructions to the four semifinalists, the chatter in the room wanes and then disappears. Lock and Wine take part in a stare down fit for a combat sport, while Spades and Purify share a warm handshake and a smile. The prior competitors are all standing in the distance awaiting the matches. The thick tension that surrounds these semifinalists makes the idea of movement challenging. Each ref positions themselves along the side at the front of each table as they ready themselves to observe the lag. The games begin.

Wine and Spades win their respective lag and both choose to break. Spades decision to break speaks to her extreme confidence. Wine has a tremendous break with two white balls being pocketed. Lock follows with a smooth bank shot setting up his next shot while burying the ball in a crowded area of the table. Spades is having no trouble with Purify as she wins Game 1 comfortably. She looks over at the other table to see they are not finished yet and shakes her head. She is not impressed with their behavior or their game up to this point. Wine pockets his next two balls, each one is a blistering shot that shows a sign of a private message being sent to his competitor. Wine takes over the round as Lock struggles to play catch up. Lock makes a valiant attempt to come back in Game 1, but he is unable to play enough defense with his ball placement to get back into the game. Game 1 goes to Wine.

Wine and Spades pick up wins in Game 2, leaving them both one game from the finals. Spades looks at Lock.

"Focus," she mouths in his direction.

Maybe this was the jolt he needed. The semblance of someone outside of his mom caring or even believing he has it in him. As self-motivated and independent Lock has always been, in this moment, it meant something. As Lock looks for his edge, a dominating Spades goes on and pummels Purify in Round 3 to complete the sweep.

In Game 3, the momentum swings, Lock pulls out a come from behind win and ekes out a victory in Game 4. Spades and Lock share a smile together. The betterment of her family will and is her main priority, but there is something about Lock that is chipping away at her normally guarded self.

Wine notices the interaction. "First, Suds, now Spades. Wow, such a playboy. And you, Spades, I'm glad to see you coming out of your shell. Just keep your eyes open with this one. You can see how he dresses down for the big occasions, but me…I'm always up…remember that." Spades' eye roll shows her displeasure for the comment.

Lock looks at Wine. "It's over." Lock's expression is cold.

Wine leans back into the air and confidently responds, "You are lucky that they changed the rules for the semifinals and finals or you would be outta here, man. You forget, I've been here before. I can navigate this. I'm glad you woke now. I was getting bored. Now, let's give 'em a show." Wine ends the conversation with a signature wink.

Lock curls his lips as his forehead wrinkles. He looks at Spades while squeezing the chalk in his hands. Spades spreads her hands out and pushes her palms toward the ground. Lock's face begins to loosen. He exhales, and he puts the chalk on the edge of the table. Lock asks the official for a minute to stabilize himself. At that moment, he feels it. The look in his eye has returned. His Spikes namesake has arrived.

Lock is in total control this round. He remains focused and quiet on the task. He remembers Sedrick's now prophetic words after the first time Haven beat him. Quiet and focused, Lock is pinpointing every shot. Haven remains undeterred. He has also double-downed, and a pin drop could be heard as the crowd watches the mastery of the competition. Haven knocks in his ball which leaves both players with two balls remaining. Lock has two choices. Attempt to knock in Haven's ball for the win but risk losing a turn which would surely secure Haven's victory, or play his ball and try not to put his symbol ball at risk from Haven.

Haven breaks the long-standing silence, "You feel it, don't you? That's the weight of the moment. I've been there. Just know, if you're good enough, there will be other times. I'm a hard pill to swallow, but you gotta take your medicine."

Lock makes his decision and takes his position. He takes aim and slightly misses the mark he wanted on his shot. His eyebrows raise and his heart attempts to break out of his chest. Haven looks on with a grin, wallowing in the fruits of his labor. They both recognize too much top spin is on the ball. Lock worries his symbol ball may follow Haven's in the hole! Contact on Haven's cue ball is made, and it smoothly falls in the called pocket with Lock's symbol ball following close behind it. The ball teeters on the edge of the pocket. Lock's ball reluctantly falls in the hole and Lock falls to his knees looking up at the decorative ceiling. Lock sees the official out of the corner of his eye. He is thinking the official is taking pity on him after blowing a big moment. Maybe helping him off the ground is a win itself. The official reaches for him and then raises his arm.

"Before the ball fell in the hole, Wine made considerable contact with the pool table. This is forbidden. Due to the nature of this shot being a game-deciding shot, Wine has been disqualified. Lock is the winner," stated the official.

Groans and cheers rain out from the crowd. Darren stays on his knees in disbelief. A distraught Haven walks over to Darren.

"Great match, D. Good luck in the finals," Haven says.

"Haven, wait! Why did you do that? It didn't make sense," Darren questions.

"I've never been in a match like that. No other reason, man. I was on the opposite end of the table, and it looked like you were going to scratch and I was going to win. I honestly couldn't believe you had choked on that shot. You have improved, I'll give you that. I got a little too excited and close to the table. I don't think it affected your shot, but the rules are the rules. I still get a good payday out of it, and you can't truly say you beat me. Win, win for me," Haven smiles and winks as he walks off.

With that hated wink, Darren rises to his feet. "Well, I did. Results don't lie!" Haven flashes a peace sign without turning around to acknowledge. Strange result aside, Darren is going to face Camila in the final.

* * *

With the finals set and a ten-minute intermission in progress, Amanda receives a phone call.

"Banks, we have a team that will be inbound in thirty-five minutes. You need to get out of there."

Amanda's agitation increases with each syllable. Her plan to cut off the head of Spikes will be thwarted with a raid.

"Ma'am, this is not a good idea. I'm too close to finishing this. I only need a few more days."

"This is above you. Your choice now is to leave or take your chances when the chaos reigns. I am warning you so you can bugout."

"They are watching my every move; I can't just leave. On top of that, there is suspicious activity just outside. There is armed security here. It is a volatile situation."

"We are aware of the armed personnel and have implemented contingencies to deal with them. If you can't leave, let me know where you will be so they can find you."

Resigned to the realization her plan has just been altered, it was time to revert to survival.

"Women's bathroom."

"Copy that… You got thirty-five minutes, Banks. Be safe!"

Amanda makes her way back to the competitors and the final table. Darren and Camila were tied at two games apiece. Amanda notices the affinity that Lock and Spades have for one another. This is a very friendly final. She is far away enough to not make out any whispers but she can still read lips. While others chat amongst themselves before the final game begins, she is watching the two finalists. Both display warm eyes and smiles toward the other.

Spades whispers, "If I see you…I will." Amanda struggles to understand the reason behind it and looks for answers through Lock.

Lock responds, "Either way, we split it, right?" Lock's smile and expression notes the playful manner and fun that these two are having even with the amount of money that is on the line. Amanda believes they have a finals deal together, but most importantly, she now understands why Lock wanted her to help out Camila's family.

"Nice try," Camila lively quips.

Amanda peers at her watch as Camila and Darren creep closer to closing their entertaining competition. Camila is in complete control. Darren has two balls on the table and Camila has one. All Darren can do is look on in awe as Camila prepares her final shot that requires her to bank on one end and travel back down to the other end of the table. The power and accuracy look good on the shot before the bank. After the bank, the shot looks less sure. It makes contact with the ball, but instead of going in the hole, it rests on the rail next to the hole. Camila drops her pool cue and briefly cups her face with her hands. Although she is a couple balls ahead, she knows it is over. Darren's face drops. He is also saddened, realizing the gravity of the situation, he walks over and gives Camila a hug. The crowd looks on in wonder. They are not used to seeing this kind of emotion. Once Darren made contact the tears started flowing from both competitors. Mark Finney aggressively eyes the official. The official then demands the game be finished. Camila breaks contact from Darren and urges him to finish it as they both wipe away tears. Darren picks up his cue and knocks in Camila's symbol ball.

Mark Finney walks to the front and begins addressing the crowd. He asks for all participants to come up to the stage. Suds heads for the bathroom when Jewel grabbed her and pulled her to the stage.

"You're a part of this, get up here," Jewel states with a loving look in her eye.

Finney explained how the top 4 participants win the bulk of the cash prize, with the winner taking home the largest amount ever received in the history of Spikes. Darren begins to think that Finney's voice sounds eerily familiar. Finney asks for Darren to join his side. Darren steps over to Finney. Finney leans in and whispers in his ear.

"You are all clear now. Fireball would be proud."

That's when it clicked. This was the man he spoke to on the burner phone. Finney is the head of Spikes. Darren is cautious in expecting any money from this win. He knows he has cleared Uncle

Reg's name as well as Sedrick's. Finney steps down and asks everyone to join in giving the competitors a round of applause for their contribution to Spikes. As he heads toward the exit, Amanda sees the sponsors begin lining up against the wall strangely. Then she notices as Finney walks out, the armed guards are coming in. She yells out for Darren and tells him to get down. Gunshots begin to fire at all the competitors and people in the crowd. The sponsors leak out a side door as the bodies fall quick and fast. The bullets continued to rain down as Amanda could feel the footsteps get closer to the stage. The FBI comes in guns ablaze, taking out three surprised security guards immediately. Amanda rises from the canvas to take out two more. Darren yells for her to get down, but Amanda has always trusted her instincts and this situation is no different. Two FBI agents go down; bodies lay still on the stage and in the crowd. Darren takes stock of the carnage around him and hopes his friends are just pretending to be dead. Blood oozes out of Camila's mouth as Darren crawls over to her. Camila could not muster many words.

"It hurts, Darren," Camila cries. "It hurts."

"You're going to be okay, Camila. I got you. Just fight!"

"Tell my family I love them, please. I tried…I…"

"Camila…Camila!" Darren shakes her shoulders hoping for a miracle, a last breath, a sign of life, but there was none. Camila was gone.

Amanda has the presence of mind during the fracas to turn to Darren to instruct him to get out of the building. Darren reluctantly heads to the exit as bullets angrily scream by in his direction. As he heads out, he turns to see Amanda pinned down by security with Amanda's colleagues bearing down on the security personnel behind cover.

Darren hears the sirens in the distance as he gets farther away from the scene. He doesn't know what to think. How is he supposed to get in touch with Camila's family? When is the FBI going to turn their efforts to find and incarcerate him? How soon can he get his hands on Mark Finney and Myron Campbell?

Chapter 19

SHOCKWAVES

I'm not a killer, but I will become a murderer. No longer can I let those empowered clowns feel they can get away with anything. I'm going to hold them accountable starting with Myron. He will wish he never came into my life.

"Hi, I'm here to see Dr. Campbell."

"I'm sorry. Dr. Campbell is on vacation, but if you would like to see Dr. Hardwick, I can get you on his schedule?"

"No, that's okay. I'd rather keep this between me and Dr. Campbell. Thanks."

So, he has bailed from work, and my mom hasn't seen or heard from him in days. I will have to get some more info before my next move. Time to go back home and see what I can find out from mom.

Usually a lengthy drive is therapeutic. This drive home feels more like I'm late for work on a day I am supposed to meet with my boss as soon as I arrive.

Pulling up to the house, my emotions return back to my purposed normal.

"Ma, I'm glad you're here."

"Where else would I be? I work to live, not the other way around. What you need?"

"Nothing much, just wanted to see Myron." Her eyebrows say enough. I need to slow down the eagerness. An investigator, I am not. "I have a few developmental projects that need to get pushed through, and I'm running into a few roadblocks. I figured he could mentor me through it."

"Ahh, that's good thinking, Darren! Myron is a thinker. As a matter fact, I just got done talking to him. Said he was going out of town on vacation and wanted me to come with him."

"And what did you say?"

"I said yes!"

"Really? What about your job?"

"Boy, I got this. I set my hours. They need me more than I need them. I just have to make a few phone calls to rework my schedule, but that's it."

What can I do to stop this? I can't kill him with my mom there. Things are moving faster than I thought.

"When are you leaving, Ma? Anything I can do?"

"Yes, we are leaving tomorrow morning. I am meeting him at his hotel. Would you mind dropping me off there? I have to be there by eight in the morning."

"No problem, Ma. Just give me the hotel, and I'll get you there."

"Thank you. With me leaving, I'll need for you to do some shopping for groceries and cook for yourself for once. Oh, and this house needs to be in the same condition as it is now, when I return."

"This is not the first time, Ma; I know what to do. You start getting ready. Tomorrow will be here before you know it."

Now, I have a window. I know where he is located, and now I just need to find a room number. I know my mom loves him, but unfortunately her son has to break her heart by removing his.

* * *

It would have been better if I didn't have these cameras around, but this will have to do. Myron is not dumb enough to ask my mom out without attempting to verify if I'm still alive. If I'm alive, he knows his life is in danger. And I like it! I have never ascended to this level of raging paranoia, and it has provided me with a heightened awareness that feels euphoric! I want him to counter any move I make just so I can show him the animal he has unleashed. The bacon covered ball is in his hand, but it is only the appetizer compared to its holder.

"I have a delivery for a Myron Campbell, courtesy of Brittany Stokes."

"Okay, sir, leave the package here, and we will ensure he gets it."

"I'm sorry, but due to the nature," delivery person leans in to the associate, "and expense of this item, I am obligated to deliver it personally."

"Give me a moment while I contact the guest."

Seconds feel like minutes as I await the outcome.

"Sir, go to the fifteenth floor, room 525."

"Thank you. Oh, do I need to check out or anything when I come back down?" A crooked look is countered by an uneasy exit. "Umm, okay, thanks again."

My patience is on trial. I wonder how Liz did it. As much as I despise what she did to me, I do understand that it was her job. She thought it was the right thing to do, no matter how many people were affected in the process. There is something to admire about that. The willingness to lie to others and go against moral beliefs for the sake of created laws and a belief in those laws versus intrinsic motivations. Truly a fascination that deserves analysis by people smarter than me.

* * *

The messenger finds the room and begins to drop the package in front of the door. The delivery person goes to knock on the door and it opens. Myron stands there with a gun behind him in his waistband.

"Myron Campbell?"

"Yes."

The shaky messenger continues, "This is for you."

"Now…it is just me and you. I know this isn't from Brittany. I spoke to her before you came up. Where is he?"

"Where is who?"

"Where is the person that sent you?"

"I'm sorry, sir, I'm just the deliver—" Myron grabs the delivery person and pulls him inside. The door remains open as he pushes the person against the wall.

"You are going to wait here while I open this. That way, if something was to happen, I won't be alone in *our* final moments."

The delivery person begins to perspire. Myron opens the small box to reveal a master lock, a cue ball, and a folded note. He knows who this is from immediately.

"What's your name?"

"I'm really not comfortable telling you that."

"Don't move."

Myron closes the door and walks over to the kitchen area and pulls out a knife. He stalks back over to the delivery person.

"I'm going to ask you again. What is your name?"

"Iago."

"Iago?" Myron tilts his head and stares down the messenger in disbelief.

"Yes, what do you want with me? I'm just the messenger."

"Don't worry, I won't shoot ya," Myron exclaims with a smile.

"That's…a really bad joke."

"Shut up! Tell me who sent you with this message."

"I don't know, I don't know! I'm bad under pressure! Look, I was told to go to a location, pick up a package and deliver it. The money was there when I arrived so now I'm here. If I would have known this would happen, I would have refused the job, but it's funny the things people leave out."

Myron straightens the clothing of the messenger.

"Leave, we're done. Take care of yourself, and in the future, ask more questions."

"That's actually good advice I—" Myron closes the door before the messenger could continue.

Myron grabs the note and makes a phone call. While on the phone, he grabs his jacket and heads out of the room.

* * *

The delivery person looks around while hurrying towards Darren in a local park.

"I'm going to have to prepare some Shakespearean scripture for you to match the *favor* you just put me through."

Darren laughs at the thought. "So it went well then!"

"Not funny, but when he asked me my name I managed a slight win by using one of the greatest characters produced in the Bard's canon."

"Wow, okay, let me guess, Shylock? Prospero?"

"No! And why wouldn't you say Romeo?"

"C'mon, Hyung. Number one, that's too obvious, and number two, you don't want to know."

"Yeah, you're right…It was Iago by the way—I don't want to hear much from you right now. I'm going home to change my underwear and rock in my chair for a bit."

Darren and Hyung briefly embrace. "Hyung, this meant a lot to me. I always could trust you."

"And you always will! You are a good man, Darren. Just be careful because this guy is scary edgy."

"That's exactly what I expected. I'm sure he'll be here anytime now. No matter how smart people are, when they are angered they will do irrational things. Thanks again, man."

The bushes wave goodbye has Hyung runs past towards the exit of the park.

The mood changes as Darren views a stalking Myron heading his way in the distance. Both are refusing to blink as the intensity grows with every step toward each other.

Darren breaks eye contact and begins to look around before addressing Myron. "I'm going to get this out of the way right now. Don't do anything stupid. We are in a public place and eyes are on you. If you choose to act on your feelings right now, I will happily put you down, believe that."

"Whoa, big timer! I knew you had some brass one's on you. That's why I'm your sponsor. I like the mentally tough. That's the only way to survive this, survive life. Your mother's the same way. Not a tepid bone in her body, but ooh, can she have a soft side."

Darren leans forward with clenched fists. He has no interest in hiding his emotions. This is his target.

"Were you in on it?" Darren directs with curled angry lips

"You serious? I am a wealthy socialite, Darren. Why would I put my life in danger like that? If I wanted you killed, I could invite you out and have someone put a bullet in your head. Easy…but I didn't, I haven't, and I won't. I like your mama. I don't like you as much, but I understand the trauma a mother goes through when she loses a son. I have seen it. I don't want her to go through that…unless I have to."

"You really think I'm dumb." Darren shakes his head in incredulity. "Like you said, you are an established, wealthy socialite. If something were to happen to you, people would notice. It is really convenient that the sponsors managed to escape, from what you want me to believe was a *random act of violence*, and those that competed didn't have a chance. That alone tells me that all the sponsors knew what was about to happen and did nothing. You knew that an attempt was going to be made on my life…and you were okay with it. So don't give me the speech as if you spared me, because you didn't. I'm done with the games, Myron. Start giving me answers or I let my mother in on who you really are, turn myself in and lay everything to bare. You have much more to lose than me. Just try me."

"You would never make it to court. Mark would make sure of that. You know what…I'll humor you and your ambitious plans. Yes, I knew about it. Yes, there is a much bigger plan in play with that move and yes, the players were the primary targets. You had to have some idea that this was coming. This was a major undertaking that should be viewed as a tree. The more this thing spread out the weaker it became. The players were simply the branches that needed to be trimmed. The tree is still there, still growing, and just as strong as ever. You may not be here to see it if you continue this foray of yours. Although you being alive is unexpected, I can make you a part of this, just like me sponsoring you put you in prime position for the tournament."

"I'm done with Spikes! Done with all of it. Your group had an unquenchable thirst that ended up destroying families. I'm not going to let it destroy mine. I'm going to do what I should have done and knew from jump, you would be unable to do…take care of my mom."

"Your mother was a necessary part of my plans armamentarium. I will admit, love was not on my mind. I didn't expect to love her, but I do now and she loves me back. Do you want to be the source behind a broken heart?"

"A broken heart is inevitable; I'm trying to avoid a broken spirit. You can't seem to understand that. You are going to help me get a face-to-face with Mark. If you refuse, I will make sure you lose your license and be put in prison for your actions."

"Sorry, Darren…not happening."

Myron reaches for the gun in his waist, prompting Darren to reach for his, but struggles to get it from under his shirt. Myron raises his weapon up aiming it at Darren's forehead. Hyung comes out of the shadows and tackles Myron.

Hyung and Myron dance on the ground as they fight for control of the gun. Darren aims his weapon in the direction of the two of them. A clear shot is not possible. A gunshot goes off, and Hyung slumps off Myron. The gun slides across the pavement. Darren swoops up the gun and sternly approaches Myron.

"Darren…it was an accident. It just went off. It could have happened to either of us."

Darren fires two shots at Myron. Myron succumbs to his body's immediate shutdown.

"I guess this was an accident too."

Darren rushes over to Hyung, scared of what he might see. Hyung wheezes as fluids ooze from his body. Darren paces as he stews over what has occurred. The gunshot has now attracted the attention of others as faces begin to multiply on the scene. He yells for someone to call the police. Darren drops down and begins to whisper a few words to Hyung. Hyung's expression doesn't change. Sirens and emergency vehicles begin to come into focus as Darren leaves the scene.

A woman acknowledges his departure. "Where are you going? What happened?"

Darren quickly spouts, "I heard the shots and found them like this. The smaller man told me that there was an altercation, gave me his mom's location, and now I need to go find her. He said he was dying. I have to go." Darren leaves the scene. He understands that things just got more complicated, and he must act quickly and independently to avoid risking another life.

Chapter 20

A SOMBER CLIMB

I have consoled my mom enough. It's time I finished this. Myron's words play back in my head, and I'm struggling to rationalize my thoughts. It doesn't feel good to break anyone's heart, but that group of elitists didn't think about that when murder became an option to their issues. They didn't show up to Camila's funeral. They didn't have to see the pain and loss on the families faces while knowing they will not mend anytime soon. I saw how much they *cared* as the "company" Sedrick worked for provided the urn for his remains. They were quick to notify the closest to kin that Haven had refused any life insurance policy offered by the company. Finney thinks he has it all figured out. His actions cloak his guilt to the unknowing, but cements his place on the wall inside my gallery of hate. He shows pain on the television as if he was hurt by what occurred, while using the forum as a pulpit to reiterate his ideals. I'm not falling for any of it. I can see right through it.

Tonight, Finney is to meet with a group of investors as he attempts to legitimize the game of Spikes. The wait is over. The time is now. I will do all I can to make sure that does not happen.

"Ma, I'm heading out." The silence makes me uneasy in an instant. It's unusual for my mom not to answer. Then again, those days are in the past. Lives have been changed, and Finney isn't the only guilty party. "Ma...Ma?

Mama Stokes responds quietly, "Alright, please be safe."

I can't avoid my mom's pain. An emotional casualty as I right these wrongs. This pain will be temporary. Those lives are lost forever. Perspective keeps me focused. I may never see my mom again after tonight. I have prepared for that. I just hope my letter and video that she will inevitably find in my room will help ease the loss. She will know why I did what I did. It will be more hurt for her, an absolute occurrence for me. Before I do, I have one stop to make.

"How you feeling?" As I look over Hyung, the cords, the tape, and his disposition doesn't look to good.

"I'm doing okay. Who knew my story would end in a tragedy? My pleasures describe my doom."

"Don't say that, Hyung. It's not a tragedy. You will recover. I'm going to make sure you get the best care possible."

"I always thought I would be optimistic if something ever happened to me…if someone died close to me, I would stay positive and walk with my head high. If I lost a limb, I would use the prosthetic proudly. But…"

"There's no reason to lose hope, man. There's too much to fight for, so much life—"

"Please! Not now," Hyung's aggressive response is letting me know I am at fault here. "I'm tired, Darren. I just want to rest… thanks for stopping by."

Mental toughness is the most important trait someone could have. It is incredibly hard to have that same mental toughness when you are the chisel chipping away at others you care about. I just wanted to let him know that I was ending this. I'm not sure he would understand. He never played Spikes. The only part he played was helping a friend in need and now look at him. One outcome is certain at this rate. I'm not going to accomplish anything by feeling sorry for myself.

Finney and Bellows Building

This is a massive building. If I can quickly find where this sales pitch is taking place, I can make this trip quick and easy. I don't care about getting caught as much as I care about Finney knowing I was the one to put him down. Entering from the air duct was never the best idea, but I'm here now. I'm already tired from thinking about all the stairs I will climb.

Entering his office, I can see an additional door along with hearing voices beyond it. That must be his personal conference room. This sweat isn't going to help my grip, but I can't calm my nerves. Deep breath and deep thought...Camila, Haven, Sedrick. Okay, I'm ready.

"*Don't move!*" My body tenses up as I feel a cold object pressed against me. Who's behind me? How? This is the worst way to go out.

"Thank you, John. I'll take it from here." The pressure from my neck is removed. Although I didn't recognize the threatening voice, this is a voice I have heard before.

"You want me to confiscate his weapon boss?"

"No need. Me and this man have an understanding...don't we, Darren?"

It's him...Finney! I could end it right now.

I turn to take my shot, but Finney slaps the gun out of my hand and throat punches me before I have time to react. Finney's quick reflexive takedown of me was not only incapacitating but also humbling.

"Darren, I get it. I really do. Let me be the first to tell you. You're not going to kill me. You're not in my league. I'm always five steps ahead, my friend. I honestly don't want to hurt you. Don't get me wrong, I did! I really did, but sometimes even my plans don't work out completely. For you, your plan failed."

I'm able to finally gather myself from choking so I can eke out a few words.

"I'm still alive, so my plan hasn't failed. I know what you have done, *Mark*. You have destroyed families, killed my friends, and you don't care! I can't wait to watch the blood gush from your head."

"First, I'm glad we are on a first name basis. You've got some stones about you. Second, I haven't killed any of my family, so that is a false statement. You think I'm an animal? Third, you are not going to kill me, but I will tell you what you will do. You will work for me."

"Not happening…I'm not a puppet. Put me in the grave or I'm putting you there. That's how this ends."

"You are so tough, aren't you? I drove you to this, of course. I made you get in this game. I forced you to take the money from the winnings, and I am the one that afforded you a better lifestyle. Did you notice that only one of those is true?"

I dash for my weapon before Finney kicks it away and kicks me in the mouth. I can feel my confidence in completing this task fading.

"After what happened to Myron, I knew it was a matter of time. I'm surprised you didn't kill him." Finney's words invoke a laser focused eye contact. "Wait, you probably thought he was dead. That look says it all…Darren, I'm running out of time here. I have constituents to entertain and sell on the future of Spikes. You are going to be the headliner. You are a natural. Don't worry, I'll market you. I'll make sure you look the part. I'll make sure Myron takes real good care of your mom once he is healthy. If you choose not to go with this agreement, I will kill your mother and then I'll kill you. Darren, Spikes is your ticket to freedom. Your uncle saw that. Hopefully, you will as well."

"As long as Myron and you are alive, the lives that are lost would still be in vain."

Finney looks over to his guard. "Okay, that is noted. John, escort him out and don't be an ass about it. He's a good man. He's just working through some things. I'll be in touch soon, Darren."

Failure! This seems to work out well for others. From the beginning, I should have known my life wouldn't be a happy ending, but it still can be fulfilling.

The guard decided shoving me through the front doors wasn't enough. "Next time you are on this property, show some respect."

Pulling myself to my feet I show him my respect with a quick one finger salute. He doesn't deserve anymore of my time than that.

What can I do to get out of this mess? I'm not giving up on Finney, but I'm not going to allow him to make a spectacle of me while Myron Campbell still dates my mother. It is time I get some satisfaction out of this day.

Walking into the hospital there is chaos on Hyung's floor. I run by his room and he is okay. He makes eye contact and looks away. I'm just glad he is okay. As silly as I thought he was at the time, Hyung was right when he said, "Worry not about the trouble you face, rather concern yourself with your face. That is where the problem lies." I need to make sure my heart and myself are always at peace. The finer details will come after that. I see what appears to be the source of the chaotic scene down a few rooms from Hyung's. I see doctors and nurses gathering around and another woman screaming. The small monitor shows flat lines all the way across. Resuscitation efforts are not working. A sad site for another lost soul. My phone begins to ring, probably my mom checking in on me.

"I took care of Myron for you. I didn't care for him anyway, hard to trust. Now, you have one move to make. I'll give you a few days to think about it. I wouldn't want you crying like your mother is now."

I look over to get a closer look at the woman in the room. It's my mom! She's inconsolable, almost unrecognizable in her pain. Myron is dead, and I can't even get satisfaction from that. I can't continue to put my mom at risk. She has been through enough. There has been enough loss. If I'm going to punish Finney, maybe I have to play things his way. I finally understand and appreciate my Uncle Reggie's message about the plant. Sometimes you do have to wilt in order to come back strong later.

If my mom sees me here, she would be suspicious. I need to get out of here. Exiting the hospital finally gives me a chance to feel again. The first thing is hunger. While eating at a restaurant within miles of the hospital, I see a family being ushered out of a house on television. The headline states, IMMINENT DEPORTATION. A part of me wonders if this was Camila's family. The light meal goes down and settles quite well to my surprise. As my phone rings, all I can think about are the last words heard from Finney. The contact on my phone says, "Sed's Girlfriend."

"Hey, Briana, you doing okay?"

"No, I'm not. It's hard, but I'm trying."

"Is there anything I can do for you?"

"I was going through Sedrick's things and found something for you. It's a large envelope, and it's sealed. I don't know what Sedrick was into, and I don't wanna know, so I didn't open it. I would appreciate it if you could come get it when you have a chance."

"I'll be right there."

My hands are trembling and my left eye twitching. Even if I don't show it on the outside, the stress is beginning to mount up internally. What could he possibly leave me? The only good news is I will find out soon. Her place is not too far from here.

I see Briana at the door and embrace her. The fresh tears are rolling down her face. She hands me the envelope and then a small box that turned up once we got off the phone. There are no words I could say to console her.

"If you need anything, please don't hesitate to ask."

A stifled, "Thank you," was all she could muster. No matter what I thought of the roller coaster ride of their relationship, Sedrick cared for her. Not all love is the same.

The anticipation is too great for me to wait to drive all the way home. I have to see what this is. I open the envelope and find a couple stacks of hundreds and a letter. I didn't even know Sedrick wrote letters. The understated wood box contained a 3D printed gun with bullets. The letter stated:

> Darren, we had a good run. I was worried things wouldn't work out for me, so I tried to think like you. Surprised, right? Well, so am I. I just want to say I'm sorry for even bringing you into this. I made things worse for you and your mom with my actions, and I'm truly sorry. Although I'm probably dead right now, you have a chance to stop the pain. I had this gun made and tested. This is only part of it. The other half of it is right outside the house address that you will see at the bottom of the page. Just go about ten or fifteen steps in the woods a quarter mile from the house, lift up the silver boulder with red

splotches on it, and you will find the rest. I think
you know what to do from there. If it's not over
now, it will never be over until you finish this. I
know you are wondering about the house. I'll say
the house contains the contents you need to end
this. I love you like a brother. Hope to see you on
the other side.

I sit statically. Then it happens. My eyes begin to swell, I feel my
cheeks shake and my lips quiver. All I can do is bury my head in my
shirt. The loss of my uncle, Sedrick, Haven, Camila, others, and my
mom's pain is just too much hurt. As the tears flow, I begin to think
about the house. Sedrick mentioned I could end this at the address
he left. He was always a few steps ahead. The pain travels to its next
destination where anger happily awaits. As my mood shifts, my only
hope is that the house belongs to Finney.

I stow the car away and wait outside the house. I wait for hours
before finally seeing a car driving through the gate. I position myself
so I can see who exactly is getting out of the car. It is indeed Finney. I
don't know why he wanted me to use this 3D printed gun; however,
when I tested it earlier I had no issues. The decorative nature of the
grounds allows me to weave in and out of cover easier. I'm athletic
but not an athlete. Trying to climb up to the second floor is not going
to be easy. I begin my careful climb attempting not to focus on the
ground with every step. The uneven stone that drapes over this castle
of a home is a great benefit for this non-climber. The success of my
climb surprises me as I approach my goal. The moon looks down on
me in shame as I reach for the balcony guardrail.

My weapon of ruin is ready to go. I peer in through the massive
drapes and see Finney head into a room within this dream loft. I just
pray the hardwood does not creek. Tiptoeing across the floor onto
the rug I can hear him rustling in the room. I picture the fading faces
of my loved ones as I aim at the doorway. I'm beginning to second
guess this. Is this what Camila or my mom would want? This questioning is what got me into this situation to begin with. My decision
making has been sketchy ever since I lost my uncle. What is taking

him so long? This will save lives. I will make sure Finney doesn't hurt anyone else. I hear Finney making his way back to the door entry. I see flashes of my mom's smile, Aunt Terry expressing wisdom, and Uncle Reggie's cool demeanor. Finney walks out the door and immediately makes eye contact with me. He is frozen as he raises his arms. He is speaking, but I can't hear him. I feel myself squeezing the trigger. A few words escape me as the shot goes off—I'm sorry.

ABOUT THE AUTHOR

James has been a fan of fiction since he was a child. As an avid Marvel Comics fan, he would try to replicate good and evil contests by pitting cereal versus milk amongst other fun adaptations that revolve around competitions. He loves sports and has participated or coached baseball, soccer, basketball, and football in intramural or playground fashion. His passion for experiencing the thrill of competition has bled into his writing of Spikes. He is not limited to stories of competition or sports. He is a versatile author who has published a variety of works to include short stories and poetry in multiple genres.

James was raised in Winterville, North Carolina, by a strong single mother. It takes a village to raise children and they lived with his two uncles and grandmother or as she was known by everyone in the community, "Mother". James and family moved from North Carolina to Portland, OR where James finished out his teenage years. After graduating high school, James joined the United States Air Force and life's adventures began. He is forever grateful for the mentors that supported his growth and the many lessons he learned throughout his military career. He retired after twenty-one years of service and continues to work to this day. He is blessed to have his champion and inspirations in his lovely wife, Michelle, and two sons, Devin and Jalen.

Thank you for coming along with me on this journey. I hope you enjoy this story as much as I did writing it. Follow me @JKWriteWay on Twitter to stay up to date on the next project and to partake in light-hearted, respectful, and of course fun interaction!

—J. R. Knox

CPSIA information can be obtained
at www.ICGtesting.com
Printed in the USA
LVHW090242261119
638546LV00001B/49/P

9 781645 844341